CRYPTID PARK

BY

ERIC S. BROWN

CRYPTID PARK

WWW.SEVEREDPRESS.COM

ISBN: 978-1-922861-81-8

CRYPTID PARK

Red eyes burned in darkness. Robert looked into them and truly knew what fear was. All his life he had heard the stories and never believed them. Those tales certainly never stopped his father from bringing him out into the woods near their farm.

Tonight started like any other summer evening, being lazy on the porch of the house, lemonade in hand, watching the fireflies dance with his mom and dad. Robert was on his phone, playing a video game instead of really taking in the beauty of it all. He hadn't even heard the first cry from somewhere in the woods that set his dad into motion.

"What was that?" his mother asked as his father leaped up from the rocking chair he sat in.

Robert looked up to see the concern on her face. His dad rushed into the house, screen door banging loudly in his wake, without answering her.

His father re-emerged with a shotgun in one hand and a rifle in the other. He thrust the rifle at Robert.

"Come on, boy," Robert's father growled. "We got work to do."

"What's going on, David?" Robert's mother demanded to know.

"That wild dog out there," his father answered. "That damn thing is what's been killing our live stock. Right now, we've got a chance to put an end to it and I ain't missing it."

Robert was staring at the rifle he had been given as his mom rose up to challenge his dad.

"You're not taking Robert with you, David," she huffed. "He's too young and it's too dangerous!"

"Hell, woman, I was only ten when I killed my first bear on my own," David snarled. "He's twelve and been hunting with me for years. He can handle himself. Ain't that right, boy?"

Robert didn't want to go with his dad but knew better than to give any answer except the one his old man wanted to hear.

"Yes sir," Robert said and then looked over at his mom. "It'll be okay."

Then he and his dad were off, racing towards the woods, with his mom shouting after them.

Somewhere in the distance, a howl rang out. Robert shuddered at the sound of it. There was an almost human edge to the voice. . .but nothing human could have made such a noise. His father picked up his pace. Robert was already struggling to keep up and failing. He watched his dad disappear into the trees ahead of him. Skidding to a halt, Robert stopped to listen, hoping to hear which way his father was heading now. If his dad zigged or zagged and Robert continued on straight, they could end up accidently shooting at each other.

David, his dad, was determined to kill whatever dog or animal was out here. The amount of loss the thing brought to their farm over the last few weeks was just too much for his father to put up with. His dad wanted the loss to end but maybe wanted vengeance even more. He was that type of guy, the kind who didn't just let stuff slide.

Robert stood listening to the night. In truth, all he could hear was his own panicked and ragged breathing. Sweat slicked his skin and not solely from the summer heat or the hard sprint into the woods. He was scared. And that was when he looked around and saw them. . . The eyes.

A warm trickle ran along the curves of his legs,

dripping onto his shoes and the ground. Robert couldn't move, breath catching in his throat. The knuckles of his hands were stark white from how tightly Robert clutched his rifle. All he could do was continue to stare into the red eyes. It was too dark to see the shape of whatever they belonged to but whatever it was, the thing stood taller than him. He was looking up into the eyes. A low, feral snarl rose from the darkness.

A thunderous blast from his dad's shotgun broke the silence. The eyes moved. Robert couldn't tell if his dad had hit the creature they belonged to or if it had been able to somehow dodge the blast that came its way. Regardless, the blast snapped him into motion. Robert while about and ran in the direction from which the shotgun was fired. He saw his dad, working the weapon's pump to chamber another round. There was fear in his dad's eyes too. That terrified Robert more than anything. His dad was a veteran who did time in the "sandbox". He couldn't remember the last time his dad had been scared of anything.

Robert watched as the beast came bounding out of the shadows towards his father. His mind labeled it a Dogman. There was no other word to describe the thing. Covered in hair, with a dog-like snout and gleaming teeth, the thing was humanoid though there was little human about it. The beast had to be the creature of the local legends come to life, real, in the flesh, right in front of him.

There was something off in how the Dogman was moving. Robert realized that his dad's blast had at the very least clipped the creature. Bright red blood smeared the hair of its right side. Even wounded, the beast was insanely fast. It reached Robert's dad just in time to knock the barrel of his shotgun skyward as he pulled the trigger. The shotgun thundered, emptying the round in its chamber upwards towards the stars. His dad grunted as the beast plowed into him, knocking him over backwards. The beast came down on top of him, its gleaming razor-like teeth snapping, trying to get at the soft flesh of his throat. David strained, putting all his strength into rolling both himself and the Dogman sideways to get the thing off of him. His desperate plan worked. The two of them both scrambled back onto their feet facing each other. David lost his shotgun as the Dogman took him down. The weapon lay between them. David knew the Dogman was too fast to allow him to retrieve it.

If he tried, the thing would be on him again in an instant.

"Shoot it!" David yelled at Robert.

Robert jerked up his rifle, leveling its barrel at the Dogman. The creature saw him and clearly knew what a rifle was. It lunged behind a tree as Robert's rifle cracked. The bullet it spat dug into the bark of the tree sending splinters flying. The Dogman came around the other side of the tree, charging at him. Robert worked the bolt of his rifle, ejecting the spent round in its chamber, and loading another into place. As fast as he moved, it wasn't fast enough. The Dogman would have been on him he couldn't manage to get off another shot but his dad was there to save him.

David slammed into the Dogman, coming at it on its wounded side. The impact knocked the beast off its course towards Robert and into the trunk of a tree. The Dogman yelped as its body struck the wood with David's weight smashing onto it. David pressed his advantage knowing it wouldn't last. The fingers of his right hand sunk into the Dogman's wound, driving upwards inside of it. The Dogman shook wildly from the pain, wailing, and then flung David from it as if he was nothing more than a child's toy.

Robert was watching it all, horrified, but when he saw his dad flung through the air away from the beast, he knew it was time to act. His rifle cracked again as he put a bullet into the center of the Dogman's chest. Staggering, the Dogman was outright whimpering now. Robert felt hope rising within him that he and his dad both might live to see his mom again. Blood flowed openly from the Dogman's chest wound, drenching its hair, and splattering onto the ground at its feet. The Dogman's head craned around to look at Robert's dad who had retreated from the beast, putting some distance between them. There was still fire in the Dogman's glowing red eyes that refused to be extinguished. Robert worked the bolt of his rifle, readying another shot. His dad remained weaponless, not willing to risk making a go at grabbing up his shotgun.

The Dogman's whimpering suddenly changed to a furious snarl as it pounced at Robert's dad. David flung his arms up to block the brunt of the Dogman's attack. Its claws slashed deep grooves, leaving spraying red in their wake as David screamed. Robert's dad wasn't about to give up though. He hauled his right arm back and brought forward a clenched fist that collided with the Dogman's snout. Blood and a couple of teeth flew from the Dogman's mouth. Ignoring all the pain that it had to be in, the Dogman grabbed hold of David, claws sinking into his upper arms, then with a mighty heave, ripped them away from the rest of his body. Robert's dad collapsed onto his knees in front of the Dogman.

"Dad!" Robert shrieked. He desperately wanted to take another shot at the beast but his dad was far too close to the thing. If he missed. . .

Robert saw the pain and sadness in his father's eyes as David looked his way at the sound of his voice. They both knew his time on this Earth was over.

The Dogman hurled David's arms away and leaned forward, grabbing him again. It yanked David's head forward and bit into the top of his skull. Bone crunched and gave way. When the Dogman pulled away, its lips and snout were smeared with David's blood and brain matter.

Frozen from the shock of seeing his dad killed so brutally in front of him, Robert stood unable to do anything but tremble as the Dogman turned towards him. The creature wasn't in much better shape than his dad. It was clear that the Dogman was mortally wounded and wasn't going to survive the night. Robert met the beast's red eyes and saw that the violence had bled out of them. All that remained was pain.

The Dogman dove into the trees, running as fast as its weakened state would allow, and disappeared into the shadows. As Robert watched the creature go, he could hear the sound of screeching sirens from the direction of his family's farm. His mother must have called the sheriff right after he and his dad had headed for the woods. Robert knew at least rationally that he should be running like hell back to the farm but instead took a step towards his dad's body. He didn't make it a second one. The world swam before his eyes and darkness overtook him as Robert passed out, tumbling to the ground.

****

Robert Jensen woke up screaming. The sheet wound about his body, wet with sweat. His eyes bugged, wide and full of horror. Every night was the same. Over and over again, Robert relived the death of his father, seeing the beast savage him with its teeth. How much was a memory of what really happened and what bits his own mind and imagination had added over the years, Robert couldn't say with any certainty.

The door of his bedroom burst inward as Iger, his head of security, rushed in. As usual, Iger had his weapon drawn and was ready to handle anything that needed to be dealt with. Iger took in the situation at a glance and knew exactly what had happened.

“Nightmares again, sir?” Iger asked with concern in his voice.

Robert nodded sharply, swinging his legs over the side of his bed. The floor was frigid to his bare feet but he placed them firmly onto it anyway. “Yes, Iger. I'm fine. Don't start wasting your breath telling me about the benefits of therapy again.”

“Well sir, it did help me out a rather good bit,” Iger responded. Though his words sounded almost like a quip, the security chief was being sincere.

“Thank you, Iger,” Robert said.

Iger nodded, realizing that he was being dismissed. “See ya in the morning then, sir.”

Robert watched Iger leave his bedroom as the security chief closed the door. Iger was dang good at his job. He ought to be given how much his services cost, Robert thought with a chuckle. He got up from the bed, not willing to face his nightmares again tonight, and headed for the shower in the adjoining bath. Slipping off his sleep pants, Robert stepped into it. The water was cold at first, making him flinch, but warmed up quickly. As he scrubbed off and ran his fingers through his hair, Robert thought about the days of his childhood. Not much of it had been very good. He'd been born to poor parents, at least by the majority of the world's standards, who were simple farmers determined to hold onto their land while struggling to pay the bills from crop to crop. His mom had been a seemingly weak willed woman who liked to act the victim all the time, to gain sympathy, but could also have bouts of rage that would leave a hardened marine running for cover. David, his father, was the epitome of the redneck woodsman who didn't know most anything about the world beyond the property lines of their farm. He was a man prone to both drinking and violence. Robert had taken a good share of abuse from David and his mother alike though deep down, in their own ways, he knew they had loved him. He might have gone on to be nothing but a farmer or a failed factory worker himself too were it not for his father's death. That night of blood and horror had changed everything and set him upon the path to become the man he was now.

No one had believed him when he'd told them about the Dogman killing his father. The authorities claimed it was nothing more than an animal attack. The media on the other hand, they fell deeply in love with a young boy who had such a tragic tale. Robert spun that notoriety into more than just fifteen minutes of fame and used it to escape the farm, devoting his life to becoming the world's leading cryptozoologist. He hadn't gone to a community college or trade school which seemed to have been his predestined future but rather attended a four year university where he exceled in several areas including biology, physics, and psychology. After six years, Robert left with enough degrees to cover the wall behind the desk in his first small office where he opened Cryptids Inc. It was an investigative firm devoted to helping those who were being troubled by monsters that lurked in the woods or haunted the shadows. The firm was an overnight success and media sensation. It quickly grew from that small office into an entire, fully staffed building in merely a couple of years. Robert invested his money wisely and hired others to do it for him as well. He was a billionaire before the age of thirty. That one building became several, spread out across the globe. Robert had always known cryptids were real thanks to his up close and personal experience with a Dogman. And just like the Dogman, so many, many other myths and monsters proved to be more than just stories as well. He never presented the press or the science community with enough evidence to truly prove the existence of the world's cryptids, instead playing the long game, building a monopoly of that knowledge for himself.

Robert was thirty-three now and owned a massive stretch of land in the most rural part of western North Carolina that he had turned into his own personal Cryptid Park. He had spent the bulk of his fortune creating it and most of the rest of his income went into maintaining it. It was his home and childhood dream made reality. Since that encounter with a Dogman as a child, Robert had wanted vengeance on the creature that slaughtered his father but more than that, he wanted to prove that such things could no longer hurt him. None of it had been easy and he had certainly made some enemies along the way. More than a few of them. There were those in the business world that he had burned badly, those in power threatened by what something like his park could mean to the world when word got out about it, and political foes who would like nothing more than to see him fall. That was why he had hired Iger and his men, to keep him safe from those enemies. Robert didn't fear his enemies. After all, they were only human. He had tamed Dogmen, captured Sasquatch, snared Skunk Apes, caged Chupacabra and Thunderbirds. . . Hell, he had even bound the Jersey Devil. Still, if Robert had learned anything over the years, it was that not leaving things to chance was the best play one could make. Iger and his men protected him so that he didn't have to worry about hitmen sent to take him out so that he could focus on more important matters.

The park was finished two years back and as of today would be filled to capacity with cryptids from all over the world. A pair of Owlmen were being delivered from the United Kingdom and with their arrival, Robert's victory over the cryptids of the Earth would finally be complete. Robert was as giddy as a school kid on Christmas morning as he thought about the Owlmen. He hadn't seen one before in anything but camera feeds and videos. The thought of them shook off the darkness of his nightmares that his morning had begun with.

Robert emerged from the shower, dripping wet, and grabbed his towel. Careful not to slip on the tile floor, he scurried over to the bath's mirror. Wiping the fog from it, Robert took a deep long look at the reflection there staring back at him. Robert smiled at what he saw. He had came so very far in life from such humble beginnings and now was his time to savor that success and bask in the glory of what he had built out here in the middle of nowhere in North Carolina.

****

Faith sat, sipping at her coffee. It was cold but she had ordered it iced. There wasn't much traffic on the road beyond the small rails sealing in the restaurant's outside dining area. The morning was proving to be a good one. The air was fresh and the sun was breaking through the clouds left over from the night's rain. This place was so different from the city Faith grew up in that it was almost alien to her. Glancing at her watch, she saw that the time was nine forty-five. Peter was supposed to be meeting her at ten but if he was anything with consistency, it was early.

A green van pulled into a parking space across the street. Faith watched as Peter got out of it, crossing the road to enter the restaurant's dining area.

"Morning," Peter flashed her a smile.

Faith matched it with one of her own. "Morning," she said. "Early as usual I see."

"Today's a big day," Peter told her as if Faith needed reminding. He looked around at the empty tables surrounding them, appearing almost surprised to not see more folks from the area out enjoying the weather. "You ready?"

"That depends. . ." Faith answered carefully.

"Don't you worry," Peter chuckled. "He's here. They all are. Howard was the last to roll into town and he got here an hour ago."

"Then I'm ready." Faith's smile grew brighter.

"Mind if I get a coffee before we go?" Peter asked.

"Knock yourself out," Faith shook her head ever so slightly.

Peter motioned for the waitress who was leaning

in the doorway which led into the restaurant proper. She saw him waving and quickly came bouncing over to them.

"Good morning, sir," the college-age brunette beamed at Peter, batting her eyelashes, likely in hopes of a nice tip. "What can I get you today?"

"A coffee, black, to go," Peter answered.

The waitress's disappointment that his order was to go couldn't have been more clear to Faith. She didn't blame the girl. Peter was more than just handsome. His Australian accent wooed a lot of women as soon as he spoke. It was like honey drawing flies without any effort on Peter's part. Faith couldn't blame the young waitress overly much. There was a time not so long ago she had been taken in by the sound of Peter's voice herself.

As soon as the waitress returned with his coffee, Peter tipped her by handing over a twenty and telling her to keep the change. Faith carried her own coffee with her as the two of them left and got into the van. Peter slid into the driver's seat while she climbed into the passenger's next to him.

The van's engine roared to life as Peter fired it up.

"It's sort of tough to believe, huh?" Peter asked

Faith without glancing over at her. He was keeping his eyes fixed on the road.

"What?" Faith shifted in her seat.

"That we're really doing this," Peter said.

"It's long overdue," Faith frowned. "The bastard should have been brought to justice a long, long time ago."

"Justice?" Peter cocked an eyebrow. "Is that what we're calling it now?"

"Doesn't matter what we call it, Peter," Faith told him, voice firm and cold, "as long as it gets done."

Peter drove them out of town and onto the backroad which led to the warehouse where the others would be waiting for them. Faith liked to think that she was the leader of their group but that wasn't the reality of things. Frowning, she knew that Brack held just as much power among the others as she did. That was her fault. It was she who located and hired him, after all. Brack was among the best in his line of work according to the underworld connections Faith made during the last few years. Still, she was the leader by right. If Faith was really being honest with herself, admitting that she would put a bullet in Brack in order to keep things from falling apart or being endangered when this close to her goal wasn't a hard thing to do.

The van pulled up to the warehouse, parking at its side door. The place looked to be abandoned. The paint of its walls were faded and vines climbed upwards towards its roof. Several of its windows were shattered and covered over with plastic sheeting. Run down would be the best words to describe the building which suited the needs of their group just fine.

Faith and Peter exited the van, heading into the warehouse. Gibson met them at the door. Seemingly always nervous and twitchy, he had his Glock 43 drawn and ready. Relief washed over him as Gibson saw who it was coming in. Faith felt pretty relieved too, glad that Gibson hadn't lost it and shot at them.

“Hey guys,” Gibson greeted them sheepishly, quickly holstering his Glock. “You're a bit early, aren't you?”

Faith, grunted, shoving by Gibson.

“Whoa,” Gibson watched Faith go on around the corner of the small hall that led into the center of the warehouse. “What’s up with her?”

“She’s waited for tonight a long, long time, Gibson,” Peter sighed and followed after Faith.

"Oh, and careful with that pop shooter of yours, man."

Gibson's cheek flushed red. "Sure thing."

The members of the rag tag group Faith had assembled for tonight were scattered about, all working on their own tasks. Everyone except Brack, that was. The professional hitman sat in a chair near one of the three jet black vans parked beside each other that they'd all be using tonight. They were the same make and model as the one Peter had brought Faith here in but these were pimped out to the max, with concealed armor, weapons, and electronic counter measures. The vehicles' engines had even been modified to have a "silent running" mode. They weren't completely silent of course but they were as stealthy as a van could be made to be.

Brack was busy fiddling with one of his FN Five-Sevens. Faith couldn't say anything bad about Brack's taste in sidearms. The pistols were famous for the punch they packed, able to blast right through most body armor and held twenty round magazines to boot. Where they were going tonight, all of them were going to need all the firepower they could carry. He must have heard her approaching him somehow over the din of the chaotic preparations going on around him because Brack's head snapped around, his cold eyes meeting Faith's own. As they did, he smiled.

"It's almost go time," Brack told her. "You sure this is what you want?"

"All of us do, Brack. That's why we're here," Faith reassured him. "And as to myself personally, with every fiber of my being."

"Just wanted to be sure," Brack said. "Once this starts, there won't be any going back."

Faith ignored that and got down to business. "Are we ready?"

"As we're gonna be," Brack shrugged. "These people around us. . . they ain't exactly professionals but I've trained them all as best I could. If things go according to plan at least some of them should make it out of this alive."

Faith knew some of the group would die during their mission. She had always known that. Everyone here was willing to do it too if that was the cost of seeing justice served and Robert Jensen suffer like they had. Still, she didn't need Brack reminding her of that right now. Faith could wrestle with any guilt over her part in all this later. Right now, staying focused was what she needed to do.

Turning to Peter, Faith snapped, “Get everyone together. I want to address the group.”

Peter nodded and headed off, yelling for everyone's attention and gathering them all up to surround where Faith and Brack were. In all, there were thirteen of them, thirteen souls sworn to vengeance and one hired killer. Only Gibson was absent from the group as Faith climbed up onto the top of a crate so that she could look down at the others. Peter had left Gibson where he was. Someone had to keep a lookout for trouble in case somehow they were discovered before their plan was set into motion. Besides, Gibson was the group's resident screw up. Whether or not the man heard what she was about say, didn't matter. He likely wouldn't benefit from it anyway.

Faith looked at the faces surrounding her. They truly were an odd band of unlikely warriors and misfits. There was Gunter, the big red head. He was a hulk. Lord only knew how much the giant could bench-press. Staying in shape was a way of life to him. Faith had once asked him about it and Gunter had answered that the reason he pushed himself so hard was to ensure that no one else he cared about would die again. She respected that.

The big red head was as driven as she was. Marcus Guffman was the next face she spotted. You couldn't get a better contrast to Gunter's muscle than the little geek. Though he was dressed in a tactical vest like they all would soon be wearing, Faith was almost surprised not to see a pocket protector affixed to it. If she was the force that drove this operation, Marcus was its brains. He was a geek to the core, with multiple degrees, and the best damn hacker Faith had ever heard of. The things Marcus could do with a keyboard would both blow your mind and scare the crap out of you. Then there was Sheena Finn, a self taught swords master, Heather Jones, their mechanic, Rick Patterson, the group's medic, Dr. Gina Fisher, a leading expert in the field of cryptozoology, Steph Hemsworth, a woman with a true passion for blowing things up, Daniel Winston, a farmer turned devoted soldier, and lastly, Joseph Rochester, a man of the cloth.

Everyone was waiting on her to speak. Faith took a breath and attempted to find the right words to convey what needed to be said.

“It's been a long time getting here for most of us,” Faith started. “We've all lost so much. . . family, children, friends, lovers, careers. . .We've suffered because of Robert Jensen and tonight, the bastard is finally going to get what's coming to him. None of what we've been through to get here today has been easy and what lies ahead will be worse yet. We'll get through though. We've planned, we've prepared, and we're ready. Tonight is the night things get made right. We roll out in an hour, people! Be ready!"

Most of those around her cheered. The few that didn't wore grim expressions of determination that meant perhaps even more to Faith. Everyone's heads were in the game like they were supposed to be. Faith stepped down from the top of the crate. Brack was watching her.

"Nice speech," he quipped.

"Meant every word of it," Faith scowled at the professional killer.

"I'm sure you did," Brack grunted. "Before we head out though. . ."

"I know," Faith sighed. "We need to go over the layout of Jensen's place one more time."

"Right," Brack nodded. "There are honestly some things in there that I don't ever want to run into."

"What?" Peter chuckled. "The mighty vampire

slayer is scared of some cryptids?"

"Don't even joke about that crap," Brack warned Peter. "That encounter with the vampire wasn't planned and my squad paid dearly for it."

"But you did kill it," Faith pointed out, knowing some of what had happened from reading the C.I.A. file she had on Brack.

"Sure we did," Brack frowned, "but I was the only member of the squad to make it out alive and it took a couple of months in a hospital to recover from that encounter afterwards. There are things in that park that make a vampire look like your run of the mill Chupacabra in terms of power."

"Marcus, Dr. Fisher, a moment of your time please," Faith barked, summoning the tech and the cryptozoologist into the rear of the van that housed the group's C.I.C.

"Yes ma'am," Marcus hurried up into it with her, Brack, and Peter. Dr. Fisher came with them too but without the tech's level of excitement.

"Call up the layout of Jensen's 'park', Marcus," Faith ordered the tech.

A map of the huge Jensen estate filled the tactical screen of the C.I.C. The size of it always boggled Faith's mind. How could a single person afford it all? Then Faith would shake her head, remembering all the things Robert Jensen had done and just what he was capable of.

At the heart of the large area was the estate proper. It was set up in the shape of a small "n". The top of the n was Jensen's personal mansion. The long part coming down on the right was home to his security staff and the personnel who maintained the estate. Their intel placed the number of armed and trained security guards at well over two dozen. The maintenance staff was smaller in number, made up of around fifteen workers. And though the outside world would never believe it, everyone in Faith's group knew that the rest of the estate was home to real life monsters. Many members of her crew had lost loved ones to creatures like the ones that Jensen held prisoner. Some of them had even been caught up in Jensen's efforts to trap the very creatures that were on the estate, used as bait or worse. The creatures, though supposedly safely held in different containment areas, were a much bigger threat to her and her people than Jensen's security staff. There was no way into the estate except sneaking across some of those containment areas aside from a head on attack straight through the main gate. . . and such an attack was certain failure if not flat out suicide. Even if they managed to break through the guards at the gate and fight their way to the house, reinforcements or the local authorities were certain to arrive before they ever reached Jensen himself.

The scariest thing inside the estate was the left building. Marcus and the others who handled obtaining the group's intel were certain that it was a cryptid containment unit for any monsters that couldn't be held in outside cells, maybe even only a single, extremely powerful cryptid. There was one section of the building that constantly drew an insane amount of power from the local grid and had, not just a single back-up generator like the rest of the estate, but two additional ones on top of that. Whatever Jensen was holding there was sure to be something that none of them ever wanted to meet. Hell, it had to be even worse than the vampire Brack had nearly lost his life to during his black op days. Their plan kept them well away from that building and Faith had made dang sure it did.

The shortest distance from the giant fences that lined the borders of the estate to Jensen's mansion was of course coming in over the hills from the north. That wasn't the plan though. Faith and her crew would be taking a less direct and longer route, coming in from east to west. This put them approaching the building that housed Jensen's security and would hopefully, if things played out correctly, allow her crew to take them out before ever making an attempt at Jensen's personal manner. It was the logical thing to do as leaving the estate's security forces undealt with behind them could lead to massive and dangerous problems should their attempt on the mansion go sideways. Of course, even the current plan wasn't without danger. They would be crossing through several of the containment areas of Jensen's park.

"Dr. Fisher," Faith said and gestured at the route the group would be taking on the screen. "Run me through what we might be up against in these again."

"Sure," Dr. Fisher nodded. "We know that the most dangerous cryptids Jensen holds in captivity are held inside the powered cells of the left building of the estate proper."

"Yes, yes," Faith urged the doctor on.

"These exterior open cells are basically just fenced off areas of the woods. Now when I say fenced off, I don't necessarily mean literal fences. Some of these cells have what equates to real life forcefields. We know for a fact that Jensen has that level of tech that he had developed for his own private use here. And some of these fields are dome-shaped to keep in cryptids that have the ability of flight...but we shouldn't run into any of those along the route we've mapped out. We will be crossing these three containment areas, here, here, and here," Dr. Fisher tapped each one on the screen. "There's no means of saying with one hundred percent certainty what dwells within each one but these cells most likely contain primate cryptids naturally suited to wooded environments. There is no evidence of alterations to the terrain that would indicate a threat level beyond that of our capability to handle with the arms we'll be carrying."

"And tell me again what you suspect the primates in these areas to be," Faith ordered.

"I think we'll see Sasquatch, Dogmen, and Skunk Apes. The last because that particular area does include both a stream running through it and a separate, large pond. That does mean there is a chance of us stumbling onto something far worse than a Skunk Ape there but I am placing my bet that we won't."

"Let's hope you're right. Thank you, Dr. Fisher," Faith said. "Brack? Peter?"

"If what she says is really in those areas, we're fully loaded up with the firepower to go through there easy," Brack confirmed.

"I can't see any issues that need dealing with," Peter added.

"Okay," Faith said solemnly. "Get together any gear you may still need to get sorted. We roll when it gets dark, folks, and once things start, there won't be any going back."

"Wouldn't have it any other way," Peter grinned.

****

Minutes after the sun had set, three black vans emerged from the warehouse. They roared along the road that led to the backwoods behind the Jensen estate. Faith's crew was split up among them. Faith herself rode in the lead van along with Brack, Marcus, and Dr. Fisher. She had some combat experience and Brack was the group's hired gun so their presence made up for Marcus and the doctor's lack of it. Plus, Faith needed Marcus and the doctor close at hand. The second van carried Peter, in charge of his own squad made up of Gunter, Gibson, and Finn. Gunter was their muscle and Finn was pretty dang deadly too in her own way. Gibson might be a loser but Faith trusted Peter to keep the man in line. The last van belonged to Hemsworth, Patterson, Jones and Winston. Hemsworth was the squad leader. Joe Rochester had been through a lot and survived it. He was the backbone Hemsworth's squad needed to hold it together if the crap hit the fan. As to Jones and Winston, in other circumstances, they would be non-combatants but tonight, everyone who could aim a gun and squeeze its trigger was going to be needed.

Marcus was busy in the rear of the lead van running ECMs to make sure the convoy didn't show up as anything abnormal on the sensors Faith was sure Jensen had running inside his estate and along its perimeter. There was certainly no sign that anything or anyone had seen them as a threat thus far or really even noticed them at all.

Brack, in the driver's seat, took the turn that led up to the hiking area north of Jensen's estate. The road was gravel and the van bounced along it, jostling Faith in the passenger seat. If she could have, Faith would have been in the rear with Marcus and the doctor, pacing about and looking over the tech's shoulder. She didn't want to do anything that would take Marcus's attention off his job though and other than making her feel better, being present back there wouldn't do anything to help. No one else in the group had Marcus's tech skills. Like Dr. Fisher, he was far from expendable. Even once they were inside the estate's ground, Marcus would have his uses. He'd hacked into the systems minutes before the convoy started its journey. Marcus didn't have full access to everything. That kind of hack would've certainly alerted Jensen's people but he had enough access to get most of the things that might need doing once they were in and hoofing through the containment areas done. He could unlock and lock doors, and with a bit of luck somewhat control the force fields around them, making sure their comm. chatter wasn't going to be picked up, and such. And Dr. Fisher was just as important, in a sense. If they ran into any cryptids beyond the ones they were expecting and had prepped for, the good doctor would be on hand to help them figure out how to deal with the beasts with the least amount of trouble.

The convoy of vans came to a halt in the large,

open area where hikers were meant to park atop the hill at the road's end. There was no one around but them. They had lucked out there. No civilians to deal with or worry about. Faith was very thankful for that.

Everyone got out of the vans. Faith felt compelled to give them all one final speech but thought better of it. The sooner they were inside the estate, the better. The three squads all headed for different sections of the high wall that blocked off Jensen's place from the hiking area.

“Sensors are down,” Marcus let them all know. “They'll be back up in about two minutes though.”

“You heard him, people!” Faith barked over the comm. piece of her helmet. “Go! Go! Go! We'll meet up at the mansion!”

Faith ran for the wall, leaping onto it. Brack still reached its top ahead of her and was clipping the barbed wire there as she caught up to him. The professional killer helped her over but stayed atop the wall as she dropped into the wet grass on the other side of the wall. She looked up, watching, as Brack helped Marcus and Dr. Fisher over after her. Marcus and Fisher looked odd in the full body tactical armor they were wearing. The tech's helmet seemed to be ever so slightly too big for him and Fisher wore hers with an obvious level of discomfort. Every member of the group, regardless of which squad they were in, wore the same make and style of armor, except for Brack. His was a lighter style of armor and Brack preferred it that way. He claimed that speed was more important to him than the protection the armor offered, trusting himself over any sort of gear.

It was all very surreal to Faith. She'd waited, worked, and planned for this night for such a very long time. . . and now it was really happening. Either Jensen was going to die or all of them were going to die trying to kill him.

****

Robert Jensen smiled, pouring himself a glass of Vodka. The Owlmen arrived without issue. They were now safely in their new home on the far eastern side of his park. The creatures were beautiful. They were just like he had imagined them – man-sized, gray feathered, and eerie. Their talons were lethal and black. Their eyes glowing red orbs that reminded Robert of burning fires. With them, he was finally content. The Owlmen were far from the most powerful or dangerous cryptids in his “collection” but there was something about adding them now that brought him peace and felt like an appropriate end to his personal war on the monsters that lurked beyond mankind's understanding of the world.

Taking a sip from his glass, Robert strolled away from the room's bar towards the vast array of monitors on its far wall. Each screen showed a different section of his personal Cryptid Park. Everything was peaceful as far as he could tell from the feeds of his cameras. The night was clear and quiet. Robert was keenly aware of the danger that lurked within the false calm of the darkness beneath the dim light of the stars. The monsters that he had contained would surely like to rend him limb from limb or even devour his soul, yet they were his. They could do nothing but exist at his whim. They were prisoners to the man who had defeated them all. Robert chuckled at the thought and took pride in his accomplishments. Not many could have managed all he had from the humble beginnings Robert had started from.

The door to the room swished open behind Robert. He turned to see Iger enter. The rugged security man halted just beyond the doorway, clasping his hands behind his back.

"Yes?" Robert greeted his scowling friend and employee. "To what do I owe the honor of this visit?"

"They're coming, sir," Iger told him. "Right now."

Robert smiled from ear to ear. "Is that so?"

Iger nodded. "Do you think I'd be here if it wasn't? I know better than to interrupt your evenings without an invite or a dang good reason."

"That you do, Iger," Robert laughed, moving to playfully strike the security man's right shoulder.

"Their cell has been after you for a very long time," Iger reminded Robert. "They're hell bent on putting your head on a pike."

"I assume they have a plan," Robert grinned.

"We believe they hope to slip into the park undetected, make their way through several of the containment zones, and eventually make a full out assault on this mansion," Iger explained.

Robert shrugged and returned his gaze to the monitor screens.

"And. . .?" Iger asked.

"And what?" Robert raised an eyebrow.

"Should I. . . deal with them?" Iger frowned.

"Ha. Not at all, Mr. Iger. Not at all," Robert took another sip from his drink. "Let them come."

"Sir?" Iger balked at what Robert was saying.

"It will be amusing, I'm sure," Robert raised his glass as if in a toast. "And it should end our problems with them once and for all."

"Oh, no doubt of that, sir," Iger assured him. "If that's how you want to play it. We'll be covered legally too since they'll be armed and a clear threat to your property and person. The only issue that could arise is. . ."

"Is the public discovering just what this place is during the course of the investigation," Robert finished for him. "Don't worry yourself there. A few well placed bribes, some favors called in and deals made with the press should be more than enough to keep that from happening. Even if it does leak out, our P.R. folks can put a favorable spin on things, I am sure. The risk is well worth those fools being eradicated and out of our hair forever. When they come, allow them entrance. Have our people on high alert and ready to take action should they survive the cryptids or begin to do any real damage to the creatures."

“Understood,” Iger grunted.

“Good,” Robert said. “It should be a very interesting and entertaining night.”

****

Peter, Gunter, Gibson and Finn made it over the wall without issue. The gadget Marcus had whipped up shut off the electricity just as promised so that they weren't fried during their climb or while dealing with the barbed wire atop the wall. They were in and now the game was afoot.

Tapping the comm. on his helmet, Peter said, “This is Beta squad. We're in and moving.”

“Copy that,” Faith's voice answered.

Peter heard the gadget that they had attached to the exterior side of the wall burn out. Marcus made them that way. None of them were stupid enough to let loose the creatures inside Jensen's estate on an unsuspecting world.

“Gunter, take point,” Peter ordered. “Finn, you've got the rear.”

The two moved to take up their positions as he and Gibson remained in the middle as the squad got moving. Gunter set a cautious pace. According to Dr. Fisher, the area they dropped into was supposed to be home to either Sasquatch or Dogmen. Peter hoped for the latter. Dogmen, in the grand scheme of things, were lesser cryptids. As scary as they might look, a bullet would down one of them just like it would a human. Sasquatch on the other hand were thickly muscled hulks that often required high powered or armor piercing rounds to eliminate. All of them were armed with M-16s except for Finn. The swordswoman preferred to carry a Heckler and Koch G36 with a grenade launcher mounted beneath its barrel. Peter really hoped they wouldn't need any sort of extra firepower tonight but it made him feel better that Finn was packing it.

Nothing had moved to intercept them as they came over the fence, cryptid or otherwise. That was a good sign. The night was clear and the stars were out in the sky above them. There was no need for the night vision goggles on his combat helmet so Peter left them pushed up. Their goal at this point was just to make it through this area to the interior fence that separated it from the estate proper. Once there, he'd send a signal for Marcus to lower a section of the energy shield that was surely in place and allow them through it.

Gunter came to a halt, holding up a hand telling

them to do the same. Peter glanced over his shoulder to see Gibson stiffen behind him. Sweat slicked Gibson's skin and he looked rather pale. Gibson seemed to at least be holding it together so far though.

“Stay here,” Peter whispered to Gibson. “Finn's got your back.”

Gibson nodded as Peter crept forward to join Gunter. The big man had knelt onto one knee and was examining something on the ground. Peter dropped to join him seeing the track that had caught the big man's attention.

“That sure as hell ain't no Bigfoot track, boss,” Gunter huffed and looked over at him.

Peter studied the track carefully before responding. “That's not from a Dogman either.”

“Then what the hell left it?” Gunter growled.

“You don't want to know,” Peter shook his head.

The track was shaped more like a hand with long, freakishly-jointed fingers that were tipped with some sort of claws or talons rather than anything's foot. As far as Peter knew there was only one type of cryptid that fit the bill for leaving a track like that and if he was right, they were royally screwed.

They had all received some basic info classes on the various cryptids they might encounter from Dr. Fisher in order to prepare for tonight but still their knowledge was limited. Peter prayed he was wrong about what the track belonged to.

"Gunter," Peter whispered. "We need to get the hell out of this containment area as quickly as we can."

The big man nodded, rising to his feet. Peter got up with him. Seeing that there wasn't any immediate danger, Gibson and Finn moved up to their position. Finn's eyes kept scanning the trees around them, grip tight on her G36.

"Wanna clue us in?" Finn quipped as she continued to look around.

"Whatever is in this area," Peter answered, "it's not Sasquatch or Dogmen like we thought."

Finn's head whipped around. Her eyes met his. There was a flash of relief followed by a new expression of real concern. Peter could see that she suspected just how much trouble they were in. Most of the group had encountered cryptids previously in their lives. That was why they were here. Jensen's people had essentially used them as bait to lure out whatever monsters needed to be captured. . . or happened to arrive during their encounter and did nothing to help. Peter knew Finn had lost her sister to a Sasquatch. The two of them were camping in the woods their father always took them to before he passed from cancer. A Sasquatch came out of nowhere, attacking them as they were hiking homeward on the trail. The beast bashed in her sister's skull and knocked Finn unconscious. When Finn woke up, her sister had been gnawed upon, entrails strewn everywhere. Finn wandered out of the woods in shock only to come upon a group of men in combat gear who were loading the Sasquatch into a container truck. She ran to them for help and got shot at for her efforts. Several of the men chased her as Finn fled. Finn only escaped by managing to take one of the men off guard, getting his knife. She'd killed him and another of the strangely dressed soldiers before they'd given up their hunt for her and rode away In the truck containing the Sasquatch. The authorities hadn't believed any of her story. They came close to charging her with the murder of her own sister before Faith showed up and got her out of that mess. Finn had joined up straightaway after being told that she was''t the only one to have such an encounter with the cryptid hunters.

It couldn't have been easy for Finn to climb over that fence tonight knowing that she was likely to face a Sasquatch again. At least, Peter knew it wouldn't have been for him in her place. Of course, everyone reacted to things differently and Finn was one tough, young woman. He'd watched her workout, practicing her swordsmanship every day since she'd joined up. She had devoted herself to being as deadly with blades as she could be. Not just with a sword either though that was the weapon most of the group thought of as being particularly hers. No, Finn was a mistress of knives too. And like all of them, she'd undergone firearm training. Peter figured her interest in blades came from the fact that it had been a combat knife which saved her life on the day that her sister died.

While Finn had turned herself into a real warrior searching for vengeance, Gibson on the other hand was simply a wreck with nowhere else to go. Peter still wondered why Faith ever approached the guy and let him into their group. Maybe she was hoping doing so would turn things around for him but losing his entire family had just taken too much of a toll on Gibson for him to ever recover. He was another body added to their numbers and not much more as Peter saw it. As to Gunter, Peter didn't know his story but knew the big man had suffered a loss in his life that Jensen was responsible for.

Gunter frowned. “I think you know more than you're letting on, boss.”

Peter ignored the big man. “Everybody stay sharp. God only knows what's in here with us.”

The squad continued on, trekking through the containment area. There was nothing special about it. The area was just a normal stretch of North Carolina woods. Peter accompanied Gunter, taking the sharp end with him. Finn held back, keeping an eye on Gibson. The guy was still keeping himself together but Peter figured that Gibson could lose it at any moment. He was a danger to all of them in that regard. The sooner they made it out of the containment area, the better.

Something moved ahead of the squad. Gunter and Peter stopped together, weapons coming up.

“You see anything?” Gunter snapped.

Peter shook his head. Whatever was out there had moved too fast to catch even a glimpse of it. That worried him. . . a lot.

“Hold here,” Peter said. The big man was clearly

uncomfortable with the order but did as he was told.

A scream rang out from behind them. It came from Gibson. A creature moving so fast it was little more than a white blur shot out from the trees, charging him and Finn. The thing was paler than hell. Its eyes glowed green. The creature gave a piercing shriek as it closed in on Finn, taking a swing at her with an overly long arm. Peter was well aware of just how keen Finn's reflexes were. Even so, she barely got her rifle swung into the path of the creature's claws. A fraction of a second slower and Finn would have been bleeding out in the grass with her throat slashed open. The creature didn't strike at her again, its claws having ruined her weapon. Instead, the creature turned to engage Gibson as his AK-47 let loose a burst of rounds, muzzle flashing. He was too panicked to realize that his shots might hit Finn too. The swordswoman flung herself flat onto the ground, cursing like a sailor. A couple of Gibson's bullets found their target despite the creature's mad lunge to the right trying to avoid them. It was then that Peter got his first good look at the thing they were fighting.

Standing up right, it would have been over six feet tall, maybe even seven. Its naked body was gaunt and thin. The creature was white as snow except where Gibson's bullet had torn its flesh. There were thick, putrid rivers of black flowing out like blood. If the creature wasn't hurt by the wounds, it was sure as hell annoying them. Peter noted that the thing's arms were far longer than a man's. They didn't resemble the overly long arms of a primate though. Its arm were more like those of the type of tall alien one would see in cheap Science Fiction films. The taloned fingers of its hands were just as unnaturally long in relation to the thing's body. The toes of its feet were taloned too. What creeped Peter out the most though was how the creature's jaw seemed to unhinge every time the thing opened its mouth. Inside there were rows of small but gleaming, razor sharp teeth.

"Watch out!" Peter shouted as the creature recovered its footing and pounced at Finn again. The swordswoman had just gotten back onto her feet. She dropped her G36 and drew the sword sheathed on her back. Its blade swept through the air to meet the creature. Finn slashed its left arm off at the elbow. The white monster loosed a high-pitched wail of pain. Its momentum carried the thing on though. Slamming into Finn, the two went down, a mess of thrashing limbs, each trying to come out on top of the other. The creature easily won the battle even with only a single arm. The backside of its right hand smacked against the side of Finn's combat helmet. The thud was so loud Peter thought it might have killed Finn outright. Still, he held his fire just in case Finn had survived it. Opening up on the creature where it was meant he'd hit Finn too.

Screaming in terror, Gibson turned tail and bolted away into the trees.

“Don't!” Gunter roared but Gibson either didn't hear him or wasn't listening.

“Hey you!” Peter yelled at the creature as it sat on top of Finn, hoping to stop it from tearing into Finn's exposed throat.

The white monster's head turned his way, its glowing green eyes locking onto him.

“Come on, you bastard,” Peter said. “Let's do this.”

The thing sprang up from Finn, charging him.

Peter was ready for it. His AK-47 chattered as he hosed the white monster with a stream of fully automatic fire that punched nearly a dozen holes through its torso. Putrid, black blood splattered through the air. Reeling backwards, the white monster collapsed into the grass. Peter wasn't about to give the thing a chance to get up. He raced forward, getting closer to it before opening fire again, holding his rifle's trigger tight until its magazine was empty. Only then did Peter let up on the trigger. He blinked in surprise to see that the white monster was somehow still not completely dead. Its body was twisting and spasming in what Peter hoped were death throes. Gunter walked over, chancing being hit by the thing's flailing arms to press the barrel of his own AK-47 to its head and squeeze the trigger. The white monster's head blew apart in a mess of black gore.

Somewhere in the distance, Gibson cried out.

"Damn it," Peter muttered, moving to check on Finn. She was breathing. That was a good sign. Just how badly the backhand blow from the monster had hurt her though, Peter didn't have a clue. All he knew was that Finn was out of it and he damn well needed her awake. They couldn't carry her and go up against whatever the monsters in this cell were too. One of the things had just come close to taking several of them out. . . and God only knew how many of the creatures were inside this containment area.

****

Hemsworth, Jones, Rochester, Patterson and Winston had came over the estate exterior fence easily enough. Now, they were hoofing it on through the woods as quickly as they could without drawing too much attention. Hemsworth didn't know if they should be wasting the time to even try sneaking through undetected. Whatever was inside this containment area was likely animal enough to hear and smell them no matter what they did. Their squad was the largest of the three attempting to converge on Jensen's manor and for good reason. Alpha squad had Faith herself leading it with the deadly, professional skills of Brack backing her up. Beta squad was led by Peter, a natural leader and the kind of clear-headed guy you could count on to get you home and was filled out by the sheer strength that Gunter brought to the table, not to mention Finn's lethalness in close combat. As for Delta squad, Hemsworth figured they were screwed because she was in command of it. She didn't have a fragging clue why Faith had placed that level of trust in her. It made no sense. Either Patterson or

Winston would have been a better choice for the job. Winston was a zealot when it came to the cause of bringing Jenson down and Patterson, though a medic, had at least seen combat up close and personal before.

“I don't want this,” Rochester complained again, jostling the rifle he carried in his hands.

“Trust me, padre, you're going to change your mind about that,” Hemsworth told him.

It had been hell getting the priest to carry the rifle at all and Rochester had flat out refused to carry a sidearm along with it. Hemsworth sort of understood where the priest was coming from but there was a big difference in using it on monsters as opposed to people. What she didn't understand was why Rochester was with them at all given that the goal was to send Jenson to hell when they fought their way into the bastard's mansion. She and Rochester had never worked closely together as the group laid its plans for tonight's assault on Jenson. She didn't know his story. And they all had one, that was for damn sure.

“Hey,” Jones shushed them. “You two might want to keep it down.”

Hemsworth couldn't help but grin at the

mechanic. Heather Jones wasn't scared of whatever might be in here with them. She could see that. Jones was just being a hell of a lot wiser than she was.

"You heard her," Hemsworth whispered at Rochester.

The priest frowned but shut up and stopped complaining about his weapon.

Patterson and Winston stayed out of it all. Patterson kept twisting his head about, checking around them for any sign of trouble. Hemsworth noticed that Winston was doing the same just in a much more subtle fashion. She was thankful for it too. This containment area was supposed to be home to a group of Skunk Apes which made sense given that it was one of only two such areas that contained a large pond and running water flowing through it. The air here was certainly more humid because of it. At times there was a sickening smell that Hemsworth caught on the light breeze that blew through the trees. It stank like a wet, rotting dog. The area was still basically woodland though. It was a forest they were marching through not a swamp. What effect, if any, such a change in environment might bring to a group of Skunk Apes, Hemsworth had no idea. If the things attacked them, she and the others would gun them down, and if they didn't, well, Hemsworth was more than okay with that. There would be enough bloodshed tonight anyway. Skunk Apes were reportedly very territorial however so it was likely that they would be attacked as soon as the beasts realized there were humans within their home.

Like herself and Rochester, Patterson carried an AK-47 too but Jones and Winston had their own taste in weapons. Jones was packing an FN P90. Made in Belgium, the weapon had a fifty round detachable box magazine and almost no recoil. The mechanic swore the P90 was one of the best engineered weapons in existence for people like herself. Winston on the other hand didn't give a crap about how well engineered a weapon was. He just seemed to be a big fan of stopping power. Winston was armed with a pumped action, 10 gauge shotgun.

Jones was right to hush them. Hemsworth knew they weren't alone. Somewhere in this area were God only knew how many Skunk Apes. She shivered despite herself at the thought. As a kid, the Legend of Boggy Creek had scared the holy hell out of her. The movie had given her nightmares for weeks and Hemsworth was still creeped out by her memories of it if someone brought it up. She chided herself for doing just that within her own mind. Nothing was going to make tonight any easier but she'd just made it worse for herself.

Patterson was on point. She and Rochester followed behind him with Jones and Winston bringing up the rear. Having Winston back there at least made Hemsworth feel safer. The guy might not be a professional like Brack but Winston knew what he was doing.

Jones, the short, redhaired mechanic, picked up her pace, coming alongside Hemsworth.

"Something's watching us," Jones told her in a voice so quiet that Hemsworth could barely hear.

Hemsworth felt it too. They *were* being watched. It had to be the Skunk Apes. The things must have sensed their presence in the containment area and were stalking them. Okay, Hemsworth thought, if the bastard things want a fight then we'll give them one.

Before Hemsworth could come up with a plan on how to draw the Skunk Apes out and engage them on her terms, the creatures took away her shot at making that happen. A roar rang out in the night.

Another followed it. Suddenly there were monstrous cries all around them.

"Here we go, people!" Hemsworth shouted. "Give 'em Hell!"

The squad fell in, tightening up their formation, with each of them facing the trees. It was Rochester of all people who fired first. The priest's AK-47 barked in a rapid succession firing on semi-auto. Rochester's bullets seemed to strike nothing but trees in the darkness, thudding into bark and sending splinters flying. Then the Skunk Apes made their move.

The smell of the creatures was almost overpowering as they came bounding out of the shadows. Some of them were huge, standing nearly seven feet tall while others were smaller and faster. The smaller ones were mostly between five and six feet in height. All of them were covered head to toe in mottled, reddish-brown hair. Their eyes glowed yellow in the night above mouths twisted in feral snarls.

Winston's 10 gauge boomed. Its blast sent a Skunk Ape back to whatever Hell had given birth to it, ripping open the creature's guts and blowing them apart. Wet, blood-slicked pieces of intestines flew through the air.

A cacophony of fully automatic fire followed the shotgun's thunder as everyone in the squad picked their targets and engaged them. Rounds from Patterson's rifle cut a swathe of bloodied meat across a Skunk Ape's chest. Jones' P50 blazed away, peppering a Skunk Ape's body with holes. Winston's shotgun thundered again, blowing the head of a Skunk Ape apart. The thing's skull exploded in a shower of red gore. Rochester was doing his best but the Skunk Ape he'd taken aim at managed to sidestep his initial burst of fire and leaped onto the priest. Wailing like a school girl, Rochester was taken down into the mud by the Skunk Ape. That opened all of them up to the creatures.

Rochester thrashed about as the Skunk Ape held him down in the mud. The claws of its hands dug into his shoulders, drawing blood. The priest's face was twisted up in an expression of pain. Rochester wasn't out of the fight though. He brought up a knee into the Skunk Ape's groin. It was a desperate move but it worked. The Skunk Ape shrieked, letting up its attack. Rochester used the moment to roll the creature off of him. It splashed into the mud but was already recovering from the shock of Rochester's crazy move. The Skunk Ape swiped at the priest with the claws of its left hand. They raked across the priest's chest. Only Rochester's Kevlar vest saved him from being slashed open. Rochester's head jerked about, eyes searching for the AK-47 he'd dropped as the creature plowed into him. Spotting the weapon, Rochester threw himself towards it. The Skunk Ape was back on its feet, closing in to tower above him. Rochester's hands closed on the rifle. He swung its barrel up and around at the snarling creature. The AK-47 roared, spitting a stream of rounds into the Skunk Ape's face. A bullet reduced the creature's left eye to a splatter of red, wet pulp. Another punched through the bone of its nose. One slammed into its mouth, ripping through the flesh of its lip to shatter razored teeth. The Skunk Ape staggered backwards and toppled over. . . dead.

Jones was taken completely by surprise as a Skunk Ape grabbed the small, redhead from behind, lifting her into the air. She brought the butt of her FN P90 down into the Skunk Ape but lacked the strength to make the blow matter despite its speed and viciousness. The creature threw her into the trunk of a nearby tree. Jones winced as her shoulder met its bark. She felt it dislocate. Jones bounced off the tree to land in the mud, rolling about there. It had taken all her willpower but she had managed to keep a hold of her P90. The Skunk Ape roared as it charged her. Jones jerked her P90 up and fired the weapon with a single hand. The creature's guts ruptured and bulged through the flesh of its bullet-shredded stomach. Stumbling, the Skunk Ape fell, face slapping down against the soft, muddy ground. Jones kept firing until the P90's magazine ran out to make sure the monster wouldn't be getting up again.

Winston's shotgun boomed as an explosion of red burst outward from a Skunk Ape's chest where the heavy slug he had fired entered it, punching a hole completely through its torso. The farmer-turned-soldier knew there was only a single shell left in his 10 gauge and he was up against two of the Skunk Apes. The things were about to rush him together and Winston knew it. Winston fired the one shot he had but the Skunk Ape he aimed at was faster than he'd reckoned. The creature managed to twist out of the heavy slug's path enough so that it tore a gash along its side rather than punching a hole through its ribs. Winston flung his now empty shotgun aside, hands going to the handles of the twin hatchets attached to his belt. He yanked them free as a wry grin spread over his lips. Winston's heart was pounding inside his chest but not from fear. It was in the heat of combat that he felt most alive, ever since Maggie had been taken away from him and Winston swore to avenge her.

The Skunk Ape on his left rushed Winston. Its right hand swung at him, claws gleaming in the starlight. The blade of his hatchet thunked into the Skunk Ape's wrist, not only blocking its attack but also nearly severing its hand. Screeching, the creature recoiled from him. The Skunk Ape on his other side had moved in too. It sprang at Winston, launching its entire body forward in an attempt to tackle him. The burly farmer leaped aside at the last possible second. Winston buried the blades of his hatchets in the monster's back, striking deep, and then yanked them free. The wounded Skunk Ape spun about to look at him with stunned eyes. He could see that the thing couldn't believe a mere human had moved as quickly as he had or attacked with such savageness. Winston ended the monster's life, the hatchet in his right hand slashing across the soft flesh of its throat which opened up in an explosion of hot blood. The red wetness sprayed over Winston. Collapsing at his feet, the Skunk Ape lay there twitching in its death throes. Winston allowed himself a full out smile at the sight of the dying monster. He heard the remaining Skunk Ape of the two he was engaged with coming at him again and turned to meet it, sinking into a defensive stance. Its wounded hand was completely gone. The monster must have ripped it away so the flopping mass of meat the hand had been reduced to wouldn't get in its way. Regardless, there was burning rage in the monster's eyes. The thing was determined to make him pay for what he had done to its hand. This time, the Skunk Ape didn't rush blindly at Winston. It circled him cautiously as if urging him to make the first move. Winston was more than happy to oblige the monster. Bellowing out a war cry, Winston unexpectedly rushed the smelly creature. His right hatchet removed part of the Skunk Ape's lower jaw and cheek in an upward swing while his left raised into the air, coming down in a wide arc to thud into its neck on the other side. Blood spurted from the monster's throat as Winston wrenched the hatchet loose. He had just hurt the Skunk Ape badly but it was still very much in the fight. . . at least until it bled out. The thing was too strong to let it really get a hold on him. Winston wasn't willing to risk that so he backpedaled, retreating from the monster. The Skunk Ape surged forward far faster than Winston expected. There was no hope of dodging it. Winston stood his ground, slashing at the monster with both of his hatchets. One thunked into the side of the monster's head burying its blade in the Skunk Ape's cheek bone, the other never made contact. The raging creature knocked the weapon from his grasp nearly breaking his arm in the process. Winston twisted, avoiding the claws of the Skunk Ape's remaining hand. He was unable to free his other hatchet from where it was wedged in the monster's bone. Weaponless, Winston ducked as the Skunk Ape lashed out at him again. Slipping under its attack, Winston ran like Hell, trying to put some distance between himself and the monster. The Skunk Ape overtook Winston before he had made it more than a few steps. Its one clawed hand grabbed him by the back of his Kevlar vest. In a single fluid motion, the Skunk Ape stopped him and slammed Winston over into the ground. The impact was jarring. Winston's vision blurred. He managed to roll over to see the

Skunk Ape looming over him. In that moment, Winston knew he had lost the battle. Winston was about to die and there wasn't a damn thing he could do about it. The thunder of a shotgun blast hurt his ears and a hole was blown through the middle of the Skunk Ape's body. Winston rolled out of the path of its collapsing corpse as the Skunk Ape thudded down into the mud.

"You're welcome," Jones told him, holding his 10 Gauge. "Reloaded this for you too."

Jones tossed the shotgun to him. Winston caught it, grinning like a maniac and laughing.

"Little red fury saves my butt," he snorted. "I gotta say that's a new one."

"New one?" Jones chided him and then huffed. "Whatever. Now get your butt up, farmer man, the others need us."

Hemsworth and Patterson had managed to keep together during the battle. Back to back, they sent Skunk Ape after Skunk Ape to hell. The only Skunk Ape left alive that Hemsworth could see was dragging Rochester away into the trees. Whether the priest was dead or merely unconscious she couldn't say with any certainty. She was afraid to open fire on the Skunk Ape though for the chance of hitting the priest. Jones and Winston were closer to the beast than she was.

"Jones! Winston! That thing has Rochester!" Hemsworth screamed.

Winston and Jones raced towards the beast. Seeing them approaching, the Skunk Ape let go of Rochester and turned to engage them. Snarling, the beast sprung at Jones. It never reached her though. The moment it was clear of the priest, Winston's 10 gauge boomed. The shotgun's blast caught the Skunk Ape in its chest, caving ribs as an explosion of red burst outward. The Skunk Ape stumbled, reeling, as Winston worked the pump of his shotgun, chambering another round. Winston put a second heavy slug into the Skunk Ape. The beast thudded over and lay still in a growing pool of its own blood.

Jones rushed to where Rochester lay and knelt to check the priest's vital signs.

"How is he?" Hemsworth asked as she walked up to them.

"He's alive," Jones smiled. "That's a hell of a lot better than the alternative."

"Thank God for that," Patterson grunted.

"Wow," Hemsworth said, letting out a huge breath of surprised relief. "We did it."

"What?" Winston cocked an eyebrow at her.

"We made it through that. . ." Hemsworth gestured at the Skunk Ape corpses scattered around them. "Without losing a single person."

"We're not out of their containment area yet," Winston pointed out.

"You're always just such a ray of sunshine aren't you, Winston?" Hemsworth shook her head.

"Just saying," Winston shrugged.

"Okay," Hemsworth nodded.

While they were talking, Patterson had taken Jones' position next to the priest and the small redhead had gotten to her feet. Patterson was the group's medic so he went about checking Rochester out.

"He's concussed," Patterson told Hemsworth. "But he's safe to move."

"Good," Winston huffed, "Because leaving him here would be a death sentence. We might have driven those Skunk Apes off for now but if there any more out there, they will sure as hell come back if they smell him."

"Can you handle him?" Hemsworth asked.

Patterson nodded. "He's stirring some so yeah, I got him."

Rochester came partly around, moaning and looking surprised to be alive. "Wha. . .what happened?"

"Don't worry about it. We survived," Patterson assured the priest, " But we're not out of the woods yet. Come on."

The medic helped Rochester get an arm up and over his shoulders.

"You good?" Patterson asked.

"Yeah," Rochester answered though everyone knew he wasn't.

"Alright then, people," Hemsworth barked. "Let's get going."

****

Faith, Brack, Dr. Fisher and Marcus made it over the fence and onto Jensen's property. They had barely started up the hill that led deeper into the containment area when Brack stopped, kneeling to examine something on the ground.

"Oh yeah," the professional killer chuckled quietly. "I'd say we're in the right place, for sure."

Faith moved to see what Brack was looking at. It was a human-shaped footprint only several times larger than it should have been.

"Wow," Marcus muttered. "I've never seen one of those in real life before."

"Brace yourself, kid," Brack warned. "You're going to see a lot more than just some prints before tonight is over with."

Dr. Fisher could see the print from where she was standing, at least well enough to know exactly what it was and what it belonged to. She was frowning.

"Fisher?" Faith asked. "You good?"

"Fine," Dr. Fisher snapped. "Can we just get going already?"

"You got it," Faith nodded. "Brack. . ."

"I know, I have point," the professional killer said before Faith could get out the rest of her order.

Marcus and Dr. Fisher were staring at Faith waiting to see who she ordered to bring up the rear of the group. Marcus' eyes betrayed the fear that he was feeling. Dr. Fisher just seemed ticked off at the world from her expression. There was only anger in her eyes as Faith met them.

"I have the rear," Faith told them. "Sorry but neither of you two have the combat experience for that job."

Relieved, Marcus fell into step behind Brack. The professional killer was already moving deeper into the containment area at a brisk but cautious pace.

“Gina. . .” Faith started but the doctor cut her off.

“Let it go, Faith,” Dr. Fisher told her. “You’ve got bigger problems to deal with than me right now.”

Faith couldn't figure out what was going on with Dr. Fisher and it bugged her. She didn't care for unknowns. They were dangerous things on nights like this one and could easily get a person killed. Her best guess was that the good doctor was either scared as crap and channeling the fear into outright anger or she was upset about the damage they were about to do Jensen's cryptids on their way to get at him. Dr. Fisher had argued that not all the cryptids they might encounter tonight would be hostile. Faith got that but it didn't matter. If a few peaceful monsters were hurt tonight she didn't give a flying flip. That would be on Jensen not them. Hell, almost all of them in the group had been hurt by Jensen and his people with only a few exceptions like Brack, who had been hired on. Some monsters getting fragged in order to bring about justice for what had been done to actual human beings was a cost not even worth considering.

The squad marched on with Brack in the lead. The professional killer's twin FN Five-Sevens were holstered on his hips. In his hands was a modern version of the AA-12 automatic shotgun. Its drum magazine made the weapon appear cumbersome but Brack didn't seem to be having any issues. From how he held the automatic shotgun, Faith's confidence in her choice to hire him grew. Brack might very well be the key to getting the job done tonight and the reason that any of them might make it out alive.

Up ahead of them a chorus of knocking noises thumped in the darkness. Dr. Fisher looked over at her shoulder in Faith's direction.

“They know we're here,” Dr. Fisher told her.

Faith was barely able to avoid shooting back a snide remark about her stating the obvious. There was no need to make the doctor more upset than she already was. Instead, she said, “Thanks for the heads up.”

Knowing the Sasquatch could come at them any second, Faith abandoned her position at the rear of the squad, hurrying to catch up to Brack.

“Stay where you are,” Faith ordered Marcus and Dr. Fisher as she passed by them.

"Hope you're ready for this," Brack told her as she reached him. "The crap is about to hit the fan."

Faith ignored the last bit and got down to business.

"Just try to keep those two alive," Faith ordered.

Brack shot her a wry grin as he shook his head in frustration. "I'll do what I can."

A Sasquatch came bounding out from the trees on the squad's right flank. Its black lips were twisted in a feral snarl, red eyes full of burning rage. Marcus squealed like a little girl but managed not to tail and run. The tech stood his ground, his AK-47 chattering on full auto as he brought it to bear on the monster. The high-powered rounds thudded into the Sasquatch's chest and upper body. Watching it all, Brack couldn't tell if Marcus's shots were really getting penetration or not but one thing was for sure, they sure as Hell weren't slowing the charging beast down. It was his job apparently to protect the tech and Dr. Fisher but Brack didn't have a clear shot at the monster. The beast had already closed in too much on Marcus.

At that moment, all Hell broke loose. As one, half a dozen more Sasquatch emerged from the woods charging the squad from all sides.

“Frag!” Brack yelled. His automatic shotgun thundered in rapid succession. Chunks of flesh and bone flew away from a Sasquatch's shoulder as a round struck it. The same beast took two more rounds to its chest. They punched through its thick muscles to pierce the beast's lungs, shattering ribs along the way. The Sasquatch collapsed, thudding onto the ground, dead. Brack had no time to do anything but shift his aim as a second beast was already dangerously close to him and closing in fast.

Dr. Fisher stared at the beasts. She wasn't in shock or even scared despite the violence that was in their eyes. To her, they were noble creatures, great giants worthy of respect. Even with her life on the line, it was hard for Dr. Fisher to harm the Sasquatch. Dr. Fisher's hesitation would have gotten her killed had it not been for Faith. The group's leader stepped between Dr. Fisher and the Sasquatch that was almost upon her. Faith had fought Sasquatch before and knew exactly what needed to be done in order to stop the monster. Her AK-47 shook in Faith's grasp as it let loose a stream of fully automatic rounds aiming for the softer flesh of the great beast's throat. Some of her bullets hammered into the Sasquatch's chin and mouth, shredding lips and sending red slicked teeth flying. Others impacted below the beast's throat but those that found their true target did the job. The Sasquatch's fierce roar became a sickening gargle. The great beast was brought to halt, hands coming up to clasp its blown-apart throat, desperately trying to suck air in through its no longer intact windpipe. The Sasquatch wasn't down yet but would be soon and was no longer a direct threat to Faith or Dr. Fisher.

"Thanks," Dr. Fisher stammered, knowing death would have taken her had Faith not been there.

"Shoot the bastards!" Faith snapped at the doctor. They were outnumbered and surrounded. Faith didn't have time for the doctor to just be standing around taking some kind of moral high ground or whatever.

Marcus shrieked in pain as the Sasquatch he'd been pouring hot lead into reached him and it took hold of his AK-47. The beast's huge hands crushed his in the process. Marcus lost his trigger finger entirely. It was torn off as the Sasquatch ripped the weapon from his grasp and flung the AK-47 away into the shadows of the woods. Marcus stumbled backwards, stunned and half-blinded by the pain he was feeling. The Sasquatch's hands came for him next. Marcus's mangled right hand went for the pistol holstered on his hip. Marcus wasn't able to draw the weapon though. All he accomplished was to smear the holster and the strap which held the pistol in it with blood. The Sasquatch's hands clasped onto the tech lifting him from the ground. The beast threw Marcus out of the small clearing where the battle was taking place. The tech's body collided with the trunk of a tree, crunching against it before bouncing away like a child's discarded toy.

Brack returned another Sasquatch to whatever Hell the thing had been born in. His automatic shotgun clicked empty in the wake of doing so. The great beast lay dead at his feet having nearly reached him before Brack's fire brought it down. The professional killer caught a glimpse of what happened to Marcus. There wasn't a damn thing he could do about it but avenge the poor kid. Brack drew his pistols with the skill and speed of an Old West gunfighter. He fired his right and then his left. Both shots hit their targets perfectly, each entering the head of the Sasquatch that had attacked Marcus through its eyes, reducing them to pulp inside their sockets. The great beast's head was jerked back by them entering before the back of its skull exploded outward as the bullets exited.

The odds were more even now. Three against three as half the Sasquatch lay dead. More even, not even, Faith reminded herself. The creatures they were up against were powerhouses of brute force and brutal rage. Faith knew she had almost emptied the magazine in her AK-47. Saving Dr. Fisher's butt cost her most of it and there was no time to switch out now. Brack had his hands full with a pair of Sasquatch that were already basically within melee range of him which left her and Dr. Fisher to deal with the other one. The Sasquatch they were facing roared and lunged at them. Surprisingly, Dr. Fisher's AK-47 opened up at the monster. The doctor was aiming at the beast's knee joints. That was a non-lethal tactic they couldn't chance taking but it appeared Dr. Fisher, while finally willing to get her hands dirty, wasn't fully committed to the notion of staying alive yet. No matter how the doctor felt about the Sasquatch, the things would tear her apart just like any other member of the squad if they got their hands on her.

Faith swung her AK-47 up, bracing it against her shoulder, as she took careful aim at the Sasquatch that Dr. Fisher was already firing at. The doctor's fire was pretty much ineffectual in taking the monster out with any kind of speed. Before Faith could get off a burst, the Sasquatch reached Dr. Fisher. The great beast slapped the doctor's rifle from her grasp and took another step closer to her. Dr. Fisher was looking up into the thing's burning red eyes, terrified. Faith couldn't save her this time around. The Sasquatch's claws came down on the doctor, slashing deep grooves from the top of her forehead all the way to her chin. The attack happened so fast that Dr. Fisher hadn't even had a chance to scream. Dr. Fisher was thrown sideways, collapsing onto the ground. The Sasquatch raised a massive foot and smashed it down. Dr. Fisher's head popped like an overripe melon being struck by a sledgehammer. Brain matter and blood exploded, squishing out from under the great beast's foot.

"Fisher!" Faith heard herself yell as if she were watching it all from far, far away.

At the sound of her voice, the Sasquatch whirled about, locking its glowing red gaze onto her. The great beast came lumbering towards Faith as she shook her head and got herself back together from the shock of the doctor's sudden death. Faith's AK-47 was still braced against her shoulder and aimed at the monster approaching her. She squeezed its trigger, emptying the remainder of the rifle's magazine into the Sasquatch. Her bullets peppered the great beast's chest with holes which only seemed to make the hulking brute angrier. Snarling, it sprang at her, huge fist sweeping in at her head. Faith ducked under its hair-covered arm and made a run for it. She knew that outrunning the beast was impossible but she didn't need to. All she needed to do was get out of its reach long enough to either reload her rifle or give Brack a chance to be able to save her butt.

Brack held his position as two Sasquatch came at him. There was no fear in him. He was cold and professional as his pistols began to crack. He fired back to back rounds into the same spot of the left Sasquatch's forehead, blowing a gaping hole through the monster's skull. Quickly, Brack switched his attention to the remaining Sasquatch, his eyes meeting the beast's. He saw the beast's rage become fear as if it somehow realized that it was about to die. With a feral grin spreading on his lips, Brack ended the Sasquatch's life with a single shot that entered its mouth and exited through the base of its skull. The great beast died instantly and sunk to its knees, resting on them for a moment before toppling onto its face.

Faith dodged again as the Sasquatch she was engaged with took another swing at her. Its claws gleamed in the starlight as they passed through the air far too close to her for Faith's liking. Desperate to buy more time, Faith swung the butt of her AK-47 upwards into the bottom of the great beast's chin. The blow didn't even seem to phase the Sasquatch. Blood still leaked from the chest wounds Faith had dealt it before running out of ammo but even they still weren't slowing it down. The monster was determined to kill her. Roaring, the Sasquatch raised its hands into the air over its head as if to bring them both down on her at once. Faith backpedaled as fast as she could, retreating out of the monster's reach. She made it clear only to trip over her own feet. Stumbling, Faith fell over onto her butt, staring up at the Sasquatch as it moved to stand towering over her. Faith figured she was as dead as Dr. Fisher. . . her plan had worked. She heard Brack's pistols barking as holes were blown through the Sasquatch's torso. Hot, red blood splattered over her from them. Faith threw herself to the right, rolling sideways to avoid the Sasquatch's falling corpse. It thudded onto the ground where she had been only a fraction of a second before. In the next moment, Brack was there, a hand extended, to help Faith up onto her feet.

"Fisher's dead," Faith told the professional killer.

"Go check on the kid!" he snapped. "I'll cover you if any more of these things come out of the trees."

Faith had forgotten entirely about Marcus. As important to their cause as Dr. Fisher had been, Marcus was even more vital. Without him, they might all be lost even if all the squads made it out of the containment areas. Mentally kicking herself, Faith hurried to where the tech's body lay sprawled out in the grass. Before she even reached him, Faith could see how mangled his hands were. The Sasquatch Marcus fought had done a number on them. Two, including the trigger finger of his right hand, were simply gone. Faith knelt beside Marcus, reaching out to check his pulse. He was alive. She saw that before her fingers touched his skin. Marcus was going to need tending too though. The bleeding from his fingers was serious. Patterson, the group's medic, was with another squad. Her plan had been for Dr. Fisher to serve as a loose medic for their own squad but the cryptozoologist was dead. She was going to have to deal with Marcus's injuries herself.

“I'd hurry it up,” Brack warned.

She knew he was right. More Sasquatch could come at any moment and they were in a bad position to take on any more of the creatures. Faith shrugged the small backpack she carried from her shoulders. Within it was a first aid kit. She hurried to stop the young tech's bleeding and get him bandaged up. Marcus jerked awake as she worked on his hands. Faith was able to slap a hand over his mouth to muffle the scream that came out of him.

“Don't,” Faith growled at the wounded tech. “I've got you, Marcus. Just keep quiet. You understand me?”

Marcus nodded his head, eyes wide with shock and confusion.

“You're lucky,” Faith told him. “It doesn't look like you broke anything when you hit that tree. Your hands are a mess but otherwise you seem to just have some bad bruises. Think you can walk when I am finished?”

Faith removed her hand from his mouth so Marcus could answer her.

“Yes,” Marcus said, “I think I can manage it.

Everything is just sort of hazy."

"That's the painkillers I just shot you up with but they should help keep you on your feet," Faith smirked. "You shouldn't be able to feel much of anything."

"Tell that to the nerves in my hands," Marcus frowned as Faith slipped the first aid kit into her pack.

"Come on," Faith stood and helped him up.

Marcus's legs trembled under him but the young tech was able to steady himself.

"I can't. . ." He started holding up his hands at her.

Faith understood what he meant. Marcus couldn't hold a weapon, much less fire one.

"I know," Faith assured him. "Just stick close by me."

"Yes ma'am," Marcus said.

Their pace was slowed by Marcus but Brack pushed them on towards their planned exit from the containment area. Faith expected another attack from the Sasquatch but it never came. They reached the interior fence. The air above it shimmered. Marcus stood staring at the shimmering air in awe.

"I knew Jensen had this tech . . ." he stammered,

"We all did but, man. . . seeing it in real life is something else."

"That's some sort of force field?" Brack asked.

"Sure is," Marcus said, grinning.

"How do we get through it?" Brack frowned, having no experience with such things.

"Just like we planned," Faith told the professional killer, nodding at Marcus, "He's going to take care of it."

Marcus's eyes bugged. "Uh. . . sure."

"There a problem, kid?" Brack glared at Faith and then Marcus.

"Not really," Marcus turned to Faith, shrugging off his backpack onto his forearm. "Can you help me?"

"What do you need me to do?" Faith asked, taking the backpack the kid was trying to pass to her.

Marcus explained to Faith how to use the handheld computer in the backpack to transfer its function over to the system of his combat helmet. The kid's helmet was unique among the group and now Brack knew why. The tech in the helmet was way over Brack's head so he didn't even try to make sense of it. Somehow, it could serve as the kid's handheld device and allow him to do the same things through voice commands. Brack watched the trees while Marcus talked Faith through it all. There was still no sign of the Sasquatch. The professional killer doubted very much that they had scared the monsters off but something certainly seemed to be keeping the beasts away. Whatever it was, Brack was thankful for it. Just another few minutes and they'd be out of the fragging containment area and not have to worry about them.

"It's done," Marcus announced. "The field is down right there."

Marcus pointed at the section he had opened for them. "We've got two minutes to get through before it seals back up."

"You first," Brack ordered Faith. She might be his boss and cutting his paycheck but it was his job to make sure that Faith stayed alive. He was damn determined to do it too. Surprisingly, Faith didn't argue. She hurriedly scaled the fence, disappearing over it.

"She's out," Marcus told him as if Brack hadn't just watched Faith go.

"You're next, kid," Brack said.

"I can't climb it with my hands like this," Marcus reminded the professional killer.

As if she could hear them, Faith called out from the other side, “Here!”

A rope came flying through the open section of the field and dangled down the side of the wall.

“Get your arms around me, kid, and don't let go,” Brack turned, taking hold of the rope. “You just hold on and I'll get us over.”

The young tech was heavier than he looked but Brack endured his weight, forcing himself on to the top of the wall and over it. Faith was waiting for them on the path outside of it. She was relieved that they had made it.

“We need to hurry,” Faith told Brack and the kid. “The others, if they made it, will be waiting on us at the rallying point.”

Above them, at the top of the wall, the air appeared to collapse on itself as the timer Marcus had set ran out and the field around the containment area closed.

“That was wild,” Marcus chuckled, shaking his head in appreciation of the level of tech Jensen was using to keep his cryptids safely imprisoned.

****

Peter didn't even know what in the hell to call the

thing that had attacked them. The rail thin, white monster was damn fast and had taken a fragging lot of rounds before finally having its head blown clean off by Gunter.

Finn moaned, beginning to come around, as he knelt next to her. Peter breathed a sigh of relief at that, not having a clue what he would have done if she hadn't. Her eyes fluttered open, staring up at him.

"You okay?" Peter asked.

"Ow," Finn reached up, her hand touching the dented metal of her combat helmet. "That thing packs a helluva punch."

"We've got no time for this," Gunter snapped. "That idiot is going to get himself killed out there if we don't save his sorry arse."

"Wha. . . what?" Finn stammered.

"Gibson ran off on his own," Peter told her.

"Idiot," Finn frowned. "Help me up."

"You sure?" Peter remained concerned about her.

"Yeah," Finn said, "Get me on my feet. I'll be fine. I have to be."

Peter couldn't argue with that assessment of the situation. None of them were expecting to encounter the type of cryptid that was in this containment area.

Peter didn't even know what the bloody thing was called but as tough as it had been to kill, they were royally screwed. God only knew how many of the things were in the woods around them. There was no chance of the one they'd taken out being the only one.

Gunter held his AK-47, watching the trees. They hadn't heard Gibson again since that first and only scream. He very well could be dead but regardless Peter wouldn't be able to live with himself if they didn't at least make an effort to save the loser.

Extending a hand to Finn, Peter hauled the swordswoman up from the ground. She wobbled a bit but quickly found her legs, steadying herself.

“You've got to have a concussion,” Peter commented.

“Does that matter?” Finn growled at him.

“Suppose not,” Peter frowned. The group's medic was with another squad so there wasn't crap they could really do for Finn given the type of injury she had.

“This way,” Gunter told them and headed into the trees.

“You heard him,” Peter clutched his own rifle tightly and followed after the big man.

The three of them moved as quietly and cautiously as they could. Gunter seemed to have honed in on where Gibson's scream came from. Peter trusted the big man to get them there.

Peter froze as he caught a glimpse of something moving out of the corner of his eye. He didn't know how to let Gunter know without letting whatever was out there know that he had seen it too. All Peter could do was keep moving and stay alert. He could tell that Finn hadn't noticed whatever it was to their right. At least if she had, the swordswoman gave no sign of doing so. Peter hoped Finn was going to be able to hold her own when the next fight came, despite her likely concussion.

Ahead of them the woods parted, opening into a clearing. Gibson sat in the center of it, torso slouched over, head hanging downwards towards his chest.

“Hey, arsehole,” Gunter called out to him.

Gibson didn't respond. He didn't even move.

Gunter stepped into the clearing with Peter on his left and Finn on his right behind him. The two of them held back while the big man continued forward, approaching Gibson.

All of it was creeping Peter out big time.

Nothing seemed right about Gibson or anything else.

"Hey," Gunter said again having gotten close enough to poke him with the barrel of his AK-47. As the tip of the weapon made contact, Gibson's body flopped over. Gunter jumped back. Gibson's face was a wreck of mangled and torn flesh. His eyes were missing, ripped from their sockets, and his lips appeared to have been literally chewed away, exposing the white of his teeth.

"God help us!" Gunter called out in spite of himself and his training, recoiling from the horrid sight of Gibson's corpse.

At that moment, the crap hit the fan. A rail thin, white monster charged out of the woods on the other side of the clearing, barreling towards Gunter. The big man swung his rifle up to meet it but was too slow. The thing was on him before he could get off a single burst of fire. The pale creature grabbed his AK-47 and snatched it out of the big man's grip.

Another monster came at Peter and Finn. Peter was ready for it though. The top half of his body turned, the barrel of his AK-47 leveled at the monster as he squeezed the trigger. A hail of bullets caused the white creature to jerk about like it was having a seizure as they shredded the flesh of its rail thin torso. The putrid black stuff that passed for its blood was splattering everywhere.

Finn gave a battle cry, racing forward. Peter had to jerk his AK-47 up to avoid hitting her. The wounded creature looked at Finn with wide eyes before the blade of her sword severed its head in an explosion of black blood. The thing's headless corpse toppled to the ground and lay there twitching in its death throes.

The creature that had taken Gunter's AK-47 broke the rifle in half, throwing the pieces in opposite directions. Gunter lunged at the monster, hoping to take it by surprise. He managed to but the monster was so fast that it almost didn't matter. The big man plowed into the white thing nearly knocking it over but failed to do so. The creature, far stronger than it looked, dug its feet into the dirt just in time to stay upright. The two of them wrestled, struggling with one another. Gunter was holding onto the thing's arms for dear life. The big man knew if he let loose, as close as they were, the monster would slash him up badly with its claws before there was any hope of getting out of range of them. Gunter heaved with all his strength, twisting, trying to hurl the thin creature over onto the ground. The creature refused to be moved, its jaw unhinging to show rows of gleaming razor teeth. As the big man was looking at those teeth, the thing hissed. A yellow fluid squirted from its open mouth directly into Gunter's face. It burnt like fire, melting away portions of his cheeks and lips. Reeling from the pain, Gunter lost his grip on the monster's arms, freeing them. The monster's jaw clicked back into place before opening again as it gave a blood curdling screech of anger.

Coming at Gunter, the thing's clawed hands staggered him with a flurry of strikes that tore through the armor on his shoulders and chest, piercing and slicing down into his flesh. The big man fell, his wounds too much for him. Gunter would have died right then and there had Finn not slipped up on the screeching white monster from behind and thrust the blade of her sword directly through its heart. Its screeching rose in pitch and then abruptly stopped. Glowing eyes went dark as Finn wrenched her sword free from the monster's corpse as it toppled forward.

"Gunter!" Peter yelled, hurrying to where the big man was sprawled out.

There were wisps of smoke rising from Gunter's face where whatever the monster had spat onto him still cooked away his flesh, gory holes that continued to expand and grow deeper. There were tears in the big man's eyes. Gunter knew he was done.

"Hang on, man," Peter urged Gunter, clasping his hand and squeezing it. "We're gonna get you out of here."

"No," Gunter coughed, blood bubbling up and out of his lips. "You're not."

""Gunter, don't. . ." Peter started but the big man stopped him.

"I need you to end this, Peter," Gunter told him, finding the strength to keep his voice level and strong.

"Wha . . .what?" Peter's eyes went wide. "I can't. . . I can't do that."

"I will," Finn said, walking up to them. She drew her sidearm and took aim at Gunter's forehead. Her hand was shaking though Peter couldn't say if it was from her own injuries or what she was about to do.

"Thank. . ." Gunter managed to get out in a pitiful moan before Finn's pistol barked.

The bullet she fired punched through the center of the big man's forehead, killing Gunter instantly.

Peter leaped up, snatching Finn's gun from her trembling hand. He wanted to shove her, hit her, yell at her, but none of that would change what Finn just did.

"He was dead, Peter," Finn told him, "And you know it. We wouldn't have been able to bring him with us. . . and you could see the amount of pain Gunter was in."

Jaws clenched, Peter gritted his teeth. Damn her, Finn was right. There was nothing else they could have done but that fact didn't make it any easier. Peter felt tears building up but refused to cry. He shook his head and turned to kick the corpse of the monster that had hurt Gunter so badly.

"Peter. . ." Finn said. "We need to go."

He pulled himself together as best he could and nodded. "You gonna make it?"

Finn flashed him a weak grin and gestured at the headless corpse of one of the white monsters nearby. "What do you think?"

"Finn. . ." Peter pressed the swordswoman.

"Yeah," she sighed. "I'll make it."

The two of them got moving. It wasn't difficult for Peter to figure out their bearings. The wall that separated the containment area they were in from the interior of the Jensen estate. Peter took the lead, constantly checking over his shoulder to make sure that Finn was close on his heels.

****

Crouching nervously in the foliage along the path that led up to Jensen's mansion, Faith kept an eye out for anyone approaching their position. Brack was next to Marcus, watching over the wounded tech. The signals had come in from both of the other squads prompting Marcus to open the shields around the containment areas for them. That was a good sign. They couldn't risk radio contact though for fear of being discovered by Jensen's security forces so Faith didn't know if anyone had been hurt or killed in the other squads. The loss of Dr. Fisher still weighed on her. Faith hated herself for that. Everyone was supposed to be expendable so long as Jensen paid for the things he had done. Yet, here she was feeling bad over some woman who shouldn't have meant much to her anyway. Sure, they worked together but Dr. Fisher wasn't exactly a close friend. Faith figured it was because she was right there when it happened, seeing Dr. Fisher die in front of her.

"Faith," Brack whispered. She heard the concern in the professional killer's voice as he called her name. All it did was tick her off even more with herself. Turning to look at Brack, there was no judgment in his expression.

“What?” Faith asked.

“My gut tells me that the original plan is screwed,” Brack said. “I think we need to switch over to plan B.”

“No,” she protested. “We don't need to do that.”

“Faith, he's right,” Marcus argued. “We lost the doc. The others could have taken losses too.”

“The other squads may be lacking the numbers to carry out the plan as it is, Faith,” Brack pointed out. “If either one of them fails. . .”

“Then we all do,” Faith frowned. “Alright. We'll switch to plan B. Marcus, send out the signal.”

“Roger that,” the young tech nodded. His hands might be far too mangled to use a keypad or touchscreen but he'd rigged his helmet to give him control over the stuff that was needed without the use of them. After a moment, he said, “Signal's sent. Now all we can do is wait.”

Hemsworth's squad was the first to arrive. They were in rough shape. There was something wrong with Rochester. Patterson was helping the priest along as if he couldn't stand on his own. Winston was bloodied and battered. Jones brought up the rear of their ragged group.

Faith breathed a sigh of relief that at least all of them were still alive. She had expected that not to be the case.

"Good to see you guys," Hemsworth told Faith, stepping right up to her and extending a hand. Faith accepted it, squeezing back tightly.

"Right back at you," Faith grinned. "What's wrong with Rochester?"

"Concussion," Patterson said as he lowered the priest to where Rochester could sit comfortably against the trunk of a tree. "A Skunk Ape tossed him around and beat the Hell out of him."

Faith didn't know how to respond to what the medic told her so she ignored that last bit and focused on Rochester's condition instead. "He going to be okay for what's coming next?"

Patterson shrugged. "Not a lot I can do for him out here."

"Where's Dr. Fisher?" Winston asked.

"She didn't make it," Marcus answered before Faith could.

"Damn," Winston frowned.

"It's dangerous meeting up like this," Hemsworth

warned Faith.

"Nothing for it," Faith shook her head. "We had to know what kind of losses we were looking at before. . ."

Faith's voice went silent as she saw Peter and Finn coming towards them. They were in even rougher shape than Hemsworth's people looked. Finn's gait was off. Something was clearly wrong with the swordswoman.

"Frag me," Hemsworth muttered, suddenly feeling much better about herself as a squad leader. She thanked God that her people hadn't suffered the losses that Peter's squad had.

"Peter," Faith rushed forward to meet him. The two of them embraced.

"We're the only ones left," he said. "Gibson and Gunter are dead. Finn has a concussion, I think. Patterson will need to check her out."

Brack grunted. "No loss with Gibson. Hell, we're likely better off without his bubbling arse."

"Hey!" Peter snapped, gently but quickly pushing Faith away, starting towards the professional killer. His fists were clenched at his sides.

"Stand down," Faith barked. "I mean it, Peter. Right now."

His head whipped around. He scowled at her but obeyed.

Peter and Brack felt no love for one another. If Peter went at him. . . there was no telling how the professional killer would handle it.

“Gunter's dead?” Hemsworth asked, stepping between Peter and Brack. Her question shut anything that might have happened between the two of them down hard.

Collecting himself, Peter's shoulders slumped in defeat as he nodded. “I'm sorry,” were the only words he was able to get out before his right hand came up to cover his mouth and rub at the skin of his cheeks.

It was Brack that spoke next.

“We've lost three people,” the professional killer said, getting everyone's attention. “Got three more wounded. Things aren't looking too good right now.”

“Brack,” Faith held up an open palmed hand at him. “We knew there would be losses. We've still got the numbers to do what needs to be done.”

“We do but not without losing a lot more,” Brack assured her.

Faith looked around at the faces of the rest of the

group. “Are there any of you who wouldn't be willing to die if it meant that Jensen would finally get what he deserves?”

Not a single person spoke up. All of their expressions were grim and determined even if some of them did look scared.

“You're all crazy,” Brack huffed. “I get all the things this guy has done but. . .”

“No,” Peter growled. “No, you don't, Mr. Brack. Faith lost her father because of him. Winston lost his daughter, Patterson his best friend, Hemsworth her father, Marcus his brother, Hell, that's the story of all us. Jensen took what mattered most in this world to us and none of us are going to let the rich bastard get away with it.”

“And who did you lose, Peter?” Brack stared him down.

“No one yet,” Peter stood his ground. “And I'm not going to. I am here to make sure that doesn't happen.”

Faith flinched at hearing Peter's response. Brack's smug snicker only made things worse. Deep down, she had always known that Peter was in love with her. Now here it was, crystal clear and in the open before her eyes. It didn't matter anymore than anything else. Only stopping Jensen from hurting others like he had all of them and making him pay was important.

Rochester had heaved himself up onto his feet. He staggered closer to Brack, stopping where he and the professional killer stood face to face. "Mr. Brack, you don't understand any of this, do you?"

"Excuse me, Father, but I think I've got a pretty good handle on this mess," Brack scowled at the priest.

"You are wrong, Mr. Brack," Rochester said, his voice strong and firm. "Like you, I am not here because I have lost anyone. I am here because the church found out about what Faith was doing and sent me to her. The evils Mr. Jensen has committed are almost beyond number but there is more to be thought of than just vengeance or the past. You see, Mr. Brack, I am here for the future. If Jensen is left unchecked, the world will pay the price for his arrogance. You can be assured of that. One does not bring so much evil together in one place without tipping the balance of the scales on this mortal plane."

"Wait," Brack stared at the priest. "Are you saying the church thinks that this guy is going to cause the apocalypse or something?"

"Or something, Mr. Brack," Rochester nodded. "While the battle between good and evil was won long ago at the cross that doesn't mean this world is beyond peril before our Savior returns. Jensen has managed what no other man has ever done before. He has captured pure evil and contained it, Mr. Brack. This entire compound is like a giant ticking bomb merely waiting to explode out onto the world. And only God knows what will be born from it when that happens."

"You're even crazier than the rest of them," Brack shot back but his heart wasn't in it. Despite what he did for a living, Brack believed in God. If the church had indeed sent Rochester to stop Jensen from loosing something horrid upon the world then perhaps he did need to be stopped, no matter the cost.

"Say what you like, Mr. Brack," Rochester waved a dismissive hand through the air. "You know what I have just told you is true. Jensen must be stopped and sooner rather than later. Every second that ticks by could be the one too many that brings this world pain like it has likely never known before."

Brack shrugged, more in an attempt to save face

than from actual feeling. "Look, I just don't want you all to die for nothing and there's a pretty good chance that you may be doing that tonight. Jensen's security forces are professionals and armed to the teeth. Our odds against them were never that good and now. . ."

"Nothing has changed, Brack," Faith spoke up. "We all knew the risks before we came in here and we all are willing to do whatever it takes. It's not on you regardless of how this plays out. Just do the damn job I'm paying you for and let's get on with what needs to be done."

Brack relented. "Whatever you say . . . boss."

****

The group split in two. Faith and Brack took half to approach Jensen's manor from the rear. Everyone else remained where they were, giving them a head start. The plan was for Peter and the other half to storm the front of the manor and cause one hell of a distraction. Brack figured that entire group was dead. They'd be up against superior numbers and firepower but it was their call to make not his.

Faith had managed to determine the exact routes and timings of the guards on patrol. Avoiding them was easy as their group crept through the trees and shadows. Marcus, of course, had to be part of their squad. His skills were going to be needed. Rochester and Hemsworth were with them too. Brack had insisted on bringing along the priest and Hemsworth was Faith's choice. Faith always respected Hemsworth's fighting skills and the woman had certainly proved how capable she was already tonight.

The path they took towards the rear of the manor led them around the building which housed the extreme power source that no one inside the group had ever truly been able to explain or account for. Marcus thought it might be the central home to the estate's control system that managed all the containment cells and security. Dr. Fisher had believed that Jensen had some sort of creature locked away in the building that couldn't be contained anywhere else and that took massive amounts of energy to keep from escaping. Jones figured the building was simply the primary power source and back up generators for the estate. Brack didn't give a flying flip as long as whatever it was, it stayed out of their way.

“What the hell?” Faith muttered to herself as she

heard the footfalls of heavy boots coming down the walkway ahead of them. There shouldn't have been any guards anywhere near them right now and so far their observations about their patterns had held up perfectly. Whatever the hell had happened to change the movement of the guards, it wasn't Peter and his squad yet. If it had been, there would have been blaring alarms and a cacophony of gunfire. No, this was something else.

"I thought there weren't supposed to be. . ." Marcus whispered.

"Shush," Faith raised a hand to silence him. "Everyone get out of sight."

"How?" Brack snapped back at her.

Faith saw why. If they just ducked into the bushes surrounding the walkway, the guards would almost certainly spot them if they came to any kind of a stop on their way through. And the woods were too far away from the walkway to even think about trying for.

"We gotta go in," Marcus suddenly exclaimed. "It's our only option."

"Then make it happen," Faith ordered.

"Yes ma'am," the young tech answered, already at work through his helmet. He was already inside the estate's control systems to a limited extent. All Marcus had to do was get the door slightly down the path from them open. He looked back at her with a grin parting his lips as that door's lock clicked. “It's done. We're good to go.”

The footfalls were drawing nearer with each passing moment. Any second the approaching guards would round the corner of the building and be right on top of them. Brack shoved Rochester towards the door. The priest flung it open without difficulty, vanishing into the building. Marcus was right on his heels. Faith and Brack had held back to make sure the others got in first.

“Go on,” Brack told Faith. She didn't waste time arguing, though as the leader, Faith had planned to be the last in.

Brack came in after her, gently closing the door. Everyone held their breath waiting to see if the guards had heard or spotted them before they had made it inside. There was only silence. Seconds ticked by like hours until Brack appeared to deem they were safe.

“They're likely gone,” Brack said.

It was only then that Faith really began to look

around at the interior of the room they had taken shelter in. The walls weren't wood or plaster but rather metal. And the small room they ducked into nothing more than a wide opening to a long corridor.

“Whoa,” Marcus said, somewhat in awe by their surroundings.

“What the hell is this place?” Brack asked, much more disturbed rather than impressed like Marcus.

“It’s like something out of a Sci-Fi movie,” Hemsworth commented.

“This is it!” Rochester blurted out. “This is where the evil that the church sent me to find is! We've got to destroy it!”

“The evil is in that manor we were heading for, Rochester,” Faith snapped. “I can promise you that.”

“You speak of human evil,” Rochester shook his head. “This. . . this is something far darker that cannot be allowed to be loosed on the world. It must be stopped, here and now.”

“Frag you!” Faith took a step towards priest as if she was about to beat the crap out of him. “We don't have time for this nonsense!”

“Make time,” Brack's words were loud and resolute.

"Brack. . ." Faith's head whipped around. She glared at the professional killer. "Whatever Rochester's going on about, it's not what we're here for."

"Maybe it should be," Brack countered.

"I am paying you to help us take out Jensen, not go on some monster hunt, Brack," Faith said through gritted teeth. Faith had put up with about all the crap she could endure.

"Yeah, I get that," Brack nodded. "So I guess I quit. Keep your money. Come on, Father, we've got work to do."

"You son of a . . ." Faith screeched, swinging the barrel of her rifle up at Brack.

"Faith," Hemsworth reached out to grab it and shove the weapon down. "Let them go. Like you said, we don't have time for this."

Marcus was shifting about nervously on his feet.

Faith could tell what the young tech was thinking.

"Not you too?" Faith stared at Marcus in disbelief.

"I . . .I just need to go with them for a bit, ma'am," Marcus reluctantly told her. "I'll be back to help end Jensen. I promise."

"We can't wait on you," Faith was on the verge of

losing it despite Hemsworth trying to keep her calm. "And we need you, Marcus."

"No you don't," Marcus shook his head. "At least not with you. I can do anything you need me to from here. Once Peter and the others start shooting, there won't be any need to stay off the comms any more."

"You coming?" Brack shouted back at the young tech. The professional killer and the priest were already at the first bend in the metal corridor.

"Just signal me, Faith," Marcus told her. "I'll get whatever you need done."

With that, the young tech turned his back on her and took off sprinting after Brack and Rochester.

Faith stood there, stunned. Somehow she had just lost most of her squad in an instant and apparently for no reason that remotely made sense.

"Let them go," Hemsworth frowned. "You can't stop them even if you tried. Besides, shouldn't we be getting out of here? Peter will be lighting things up out there soon."

Defeated, Faith's shoulders slumped. "Yeah. . . We best be about it."

The two women quietly opened the door they had all entered through and emerged out onto the walkway. There were no signs of any guards. Hemsworth took the lead, heading on along their planned path towards the rear of Jensen's manor. Faith followed after her, still wondering how everything had spun so out of control so quickly.

****

Iger paced back and forth in the estate's main security room on the first floor of Jensen's manor. The tension in his muscles had been building since the first group of intruders scaled the exterior fence. He wanted desperately to engage them but couldn't. Jensen's updated orders were very clear. There was to be no intentional contact with the intruders until they made their move on the manor itself or did something to endanger the Omega level containment cell in Building C. A was the main itself, B was home to the estate's staff and security. Building C was entirely devoted to keeping the cryptid within it from breaking free. Iger had never seen the thing with his own eyes but he had heard enough from the few of his men that had to know he didn't want to. Since the cryptid had been imprisoned there, two of his men and three of the "science" staff were let go and sent off to mental hospitals after working in the building. An engineer flat out died in there without any logical explanation. Iger saw that woman's body before the ambulance drove away with it. Her sunken eyes still haunted Iger in his nightmares. Before the medical people zipped up her body bag, Iger got a good look at what became of her. The woman's skin was pulled tight to her bones as if everything between them were simply gone. It made Iger think of someone who died from a long and painful hunger as their body consumed itself to stay alive until there was nothing left. There wasn't a single mark or wound upon her stretched tight flesh. Iger had never seen anything like it in his life, considering that the engineer was fine that morning before heading into the building to make some upgrades and run some system checks on the Omega level containment cell. Whatever happened to her must have happened fast because her face was forever locked in a terrified scream, mouth open and sunken eyes wide. Iger forced those memories away. He needed to stay focused. There were foxes in his henhouse and Iger would be damned if he didn't stop them. Why Jensen wanted them to have a free run up to the manor itself didn't make much sense.

The monitors on the walls showed images from the concealed cameras around the position where half of the surviving members of the bastards who had broken into the estate were preparing to do something really stupid. From the looks of things, they were preparing to make a full out frontal assault on the front of the manor despite being vastly outnumbered and outgunned. Their plan must be to draw attention to themselves so that the other half of them could move about more freely and perhaps not be noticed. Unfortunately for them, Iger already knew exactly where the others were and where they were headed. Serving themselves up to die wouldn't help their friends at all but it would finally let him go at them like he wanted to.

Returning his attention to the half of the group heading for the rear of the manor, Iger realized with a start that they had disappeared from the cameras. He found them hiding as some of his guards approached their position. Rather than engage his people, the intruders ducked into Building C through one of its side maintenance doors. Iger shuddered as a chill ran along his back and down his arms. His people passed on by without ever knowing the intruders were there but. . . the intruders didn't come out of Building C, at least not at first. Iger watched and waited for them to emerge before his worst fear took place before his eyes. When the intruders did exit Building C, it was only two of them. The other three had stayed inside. Iger swallowed hard. They couldn't be allowed to remain in the building. He was going to have to send people in after them. The risk of doing that was terrible but what else could he do? Leave what happened to the fools to chance? If they let loose the creature inside there, they would be just as dead as if his men took them out. The thought of that thing being loosed made Iger shudder again.

"Samantha!" Iger barked.

She stood by the entrance to the control room but came rushing to him at the sound of her name. Samantha was only five foot three but Iger was well aware of what a powerhouse of fury the woman was. She was one of his best and he didn't dare trust anyone else with the job he was about to give her.

"Sir!" Samantha said, coming to a halt in front of him, standing at attention.

"Some of the intruders have gone into Building C. I need you to take five or six people, ones that can be trusted not to be too trigger happy, in there, and go make sure the bastards find their way out, preferably in body bags."

"Yes sir," Samantha gave a sharp nod.

Iger watched her exit the control room to carry out the orders she had just been given. If anyone could deal with the intruders without letting that thing in Building C loose, it was Samantha. With that situation dealt with as best as it could be, Iger was glad that the rest of the intruders were about to give him something to do and take his mind off that entire mess for a bit.

The half of the group out front were just about to make their move. Iger used the tactical frequency the helmets of his people in that area were set to. "It's time. When they start things, I want you guys to end it."

****

Peter looked at the others with him – Winston, Patterson, Finn, and Jones. Patterson was a fragging medic, Jones, no matter how tough he was, a mechanic, and Finn was injured. Winston was the only real fighter among them and even he wasn't truly a professional like the men and women they were about to be trading bullets with. Still, there was nothing for it. The job needed to be done and it was up to them.

In his backpack was a modified M72 L.A.W. Peter got the weapon out and readied it for use, loading up the only rocket he had. They all knew it would take serious firepower to pierce the main doors of the manor and that was what the rocket was to be used for. He was within range so Peter figured doing so would be a hell of a way to kick off the diversion that Faith and her squad were counting on him to cause.

Before bringing the L.A.W. up to his shoulder, Peter signaled at Winston who nodded in response. It was time. Peter took aim at the main door of the manor and took his shot. The rocket exploded out of the launcher, streaking straight into its target. There were two guards posted outside the door. One of them died instantly from the blast as the rocket slammed into the door and the concussive wave shattered the bones of his body. The other guard was flung forward, loosing his weapon, his right arm snapping beneath the weight of his own body as he landed hard on the concrete walkway leading up to the door. The door wasn't destroyed or blown apart. It was too well made and tough for that but it did buckle in its frame to where it could easily be kicked down. Then all hell broke loose.

“We're under attack!” a security officer wailed.

“Take cover!” another cried out.

Peter tapped his helmet's comlink. “Hit 'em.”

Winston had traded his combat shotgun for the standard AK-47 the group used. He swept the front of the manor where the guards were darting about in utter chaos with a stream of fully automatic fire. Patterson opened up too. Finn and Jones were positioned back from them and for the time being kept out of the fight. The odds were that those in front of them would be forced to fallback rather than be able to push forward towards the manor. When they did, they'd act. Peter's plan was for those coming after them to run straight into their line of fire.

Guards came from seemingly everywhere. Peter grimaced at how many there were. Winston and Patterson were laying down a heavy barrage of rounds but it wasn't enough. A guard shrieked and died as Winston put half a dozen bullets in the man's chest. Another tumbled as his legs were shredded by Patterson. Peter realized that Patterson wasn’t shooting to kill. Well, frag, Peter thought but right now, as long as Patterson was at least in the fight, it was a hell of a lot better to have him than not.

A guard came running towards where the three of them were making their stand. Winston took the woman out but not before she accomplished what she had intended. A grenade flew at Patterson and Winston on an arc to land between them.

"Oh shi. . ." Patterson managed to get out before the grenade detonated.

The blast filled the medic's lower body with shards of metal. They slashed and sliced the flesh of his legs, shredding his genitals. Patterson collapsed, bleeding heavily, knocked out from the shock of the severe pain that racked his body.

Winston was luckier than the medic, able to duck around the side of the bush he was using as cover to somewhat protect himself from the blast.

"Patterson!" Winston shouted. He started towards where the medic lay but gunfire from several of the guards forced him into retreat. Winston took cover again, watching as Peter tried to reach the medic too. He didn't make it either. They both could see that Patterson was either already dead or unconscious. There was no hope of knowing which without getting closer to him.

Peter knew he had a tough call to make. The guards were pressing in fast. If they didn't move, the battle might end a lot quicker than any of them thought it would but if they did, it meant leaving the medic behind. Peter cursed, ducking a bullet which thudded into the wood of the small tree he was using for cover. They stung his face, tearing into his skin. Beads of blood from the tiny wounds ran down his cheeks and forehead like sweat. In that moment, Peter knew the truth of the situation and the choice had already been made for him. He and Winston were far too out-matched.

“Fallback!” Peter yelled, abandoning what cover he had to make a run for it.

Winston heard him and bugged out too. They zigged and zagged through the few trees of the landscape directly in front of the manor. The guards pursued them, guns blazing. Peter almost forgot about the plan entirely in his panic. The roar of Jones and Finn's AK-47s opening up on the group of guards behind him and Winston caught Peter by surprise. The two women sent several of the guards to hell before the others even realized they had been led into a trap.

The mad charge of the guards pursuing them was

broken. They scattered in search of cover and began returning fire at Jones and Finn. Peter broke in the direction of Finn while Winston headed for where Jones was hunched behind the statue of a tentacled cryptid of some kind.

“Patterson?” Finn asked as Peter joined her in the bushes she was using for cover.

“Dead,” Peter grunted. “We're gonna be too if we don't get the hell out of here.”

“No argument here,” Finn flashed a wry grin at him.

“Jones, Winston,” Peter said over his helmet's comm. “Hone in on this signal and get to us as quick as you can.”

“Copy that,” Winston's deep, rough voice responded.

Peter laid down cover fire, allowing Finn to break from their cover first. If he recalled the layout of the front of the estate correctly there were multiple garages ahead of them. Getting their hands on a vehicle could greatly increase the odds of any of them making it out alive. His legs pumped under him, breaths coming in ragged gasps, as Peter pushed himself to overtake and pass Finn. For a woman with a head injury, she was hanging in there a hell of a lot better than he had expected she would. As he passed by Finn, taking the lead, Peter headed towards the cluster of small buildings up ahead to their right. None of them were big enough to have been counted as true buildings while they were planning the attack on the manor given how large the main three in the estate's center were.

"This way!" Peter yelled over his shoulder and pushed himself on even faster.

****

"This place is insane," Marcus said more to himself than either Brack or Rochester.

Brack agreed with the young tech though he said nothing. The long corridor they walked along was more like the inside of some sort of vast spaceship than anything that should be found inside a building in western North Carolina. Brack had seen a hell of a lot of things in his career but nothing ever like this. He reached out and ran his fingers over the cold metal of the corridor's wall. Yeah, shooting in here could be dangerous. Ricochets could be deadly bouncing everywhere.

"We're getting closer," Rochester announced.

"How do you know that?" Marcus asked. "The

system in here is so heavily encrypted I can't get any info out of it except that this place is indeed a holding cell for a cryptid of incredible power. It's like even Jensen is scared to death of it. I mean, why else would he build a place like this?"

"A better question would be how the hell did he manage to trap whatever this place is holding and bring it here anyway?" Brack looked to Rochester for an answer.

"Maybe he didn't, Mr. Brack," The priest said. "Perhaps the thing contained within this place wanted to come here."

"Let's not jump to hasty conclusions," Marcus cautioned. "With the level of resources Jensen has at his disposal who is to say what the guy can and can't pull off. I mean, think about it. This whole estate is a testament to that."

"And you have no idea what this creature is?" Brack asked Rochester.

The priest shook his head. "I can tell you it is evil incarnate, Mr. Brack, and that it is very, very hungry."

"Real helpful," Brack frowned.

"Ain't it, though?" Marcus quipped with an intentional Southern accent.

The trio reached the end of the corridor. A door was waiting for them there. It wasn't like the others that seemed to be junction points. No, this one was far denser and heavier in its structure. Brack didn't want to find out what was behind it but knew he had to.

"I'd say we've found what we're looking for," Brack rapped his knuckles against the metal of the door. "Marcus?"

"I'm trying," the young tech answered. "Like I said, thc system in this building is way more advanced and tight than the rest of the estate. It may take me a bit."

"The clock is ticking," Brack reminded him.

"That isn't exactly helpful," Marcus scowled at the professional killer.

"Just get it done," Brack ordered.

Rochester wore a necklace about his neck that contained a silver cross. The priest had taken the cross out from beneath his shirt and held it with both hands, whispering the words of a prayer that Brack couldn't hear.

"You really think that's going to help?" Brack asked though he didn't tell Rochester to stop.

The priest's head rose up from his prayer.

Rochester met Brack's eyes. “God has led us here, Mr. Brack. We are who He has chosen to confront the evil behind that door and ensure that it is stopped.”

“That evil wasn't always locked up, Rochester,” Brack pointed out. “It was already loose once.”

“Yes. You are correct,” the priest nodded. “But then it was not as . . . focused as it has become now in Jensen’s hands.”

“What does that even mean?” Brack asked.

“I don’t fully understand it myself, Mr. Brack, nor do I pretend to,” Rochester's hands still clutched the silver cross they held so tightly that his knuckles were white as snow. “What I do know is what I have told you. It must be stopped and now. If we fail, the world will pay the price.”

“Got it!” Marcus blurted out. Heavy motors inside the frame of the door roared to life. The door parted in its center, sliding open. The room beyond it was dimmer than the corridor they were in. A deep wave of cold washed over all three of them. Marcus and Brack shuddered. Rochester either didn't feel it or ignored the cold, walking straight on into the room.

The room was wide. There were work stations

and what appeared to be monitoring stations that ran around the curve of its circular shape. In the room's center sat a massive tank. A horrid, utterly inhuman shrieking came from within it though nothing could be seen. The tank was filled with a swirling, gray cloud or fog that never stopped moving. It obscured whatever the source of the sound was. The trio all stood staring at the tank, transfixed by it.

Brack shook his head to clear it as Rochester fell to his knees. The priest had his silver cross again in his hands, chanting a prayer in Latin. Brack had no idea what the priest was saying but whatever it was, fear tinged Rochester's voice and the prayer was as passionate as they came.

"Whoa," Marcus breathed. He didn't know what to make of the tank or its mysterious occupant but it was affecting him nonetheless. The young tech was pale and frozen to the spot where he stood. It was as if a supernatural force was reaching out from within the tank, chilling them all to the bone. Marcus shivered. He checked the room's control systems through what limited access was available to him only to find that it wasn't supposed to be cold. According to the data, the room should be a comfortable seventy-four degrees.

“So that's it?” Brack asked. “The thing we're after?”

Rochester was so out of his head that the priest didn't answer him. He just kept praying, the necklace around his neck shaking from the trembling of his hands as they clutched the cross attached to it.

“Okay,” Brack turned to Marcus. The young tech's eyes were wide and his brow furrowed in thought. “Rochester's lost it. What do you got, kid?”

“I. . .I . . .” Marcus stammered.

“Come on, kid,” Brack pressed him then redirected his original question. “Is that the thing we're after?”

“Yeah,” Marcus nodded slowly. “I think so anyway.”

“Can you tell me what it is?” Brack stepped closer to Marcus as the young tech moved to one of the consoles that ran in a circle surrounding the tank.

“No,” Marcus answered. “Not really. I can tell you it's not like a Sasquatch, Skunk Ape, or Thunderbird. Whatever is in there. . .” Marcus raised a wounded hand to point at the tank. “It's supernatural.”

Brack eyed the young tech and saw that he was

telling the truth. He felt it too. The cold, the presence of evil, every instinct in his body telling him to run like hell as far as he could get from the thing in the tank.

"Any ideas on how we kill it?" Brack asked.

Marcus shook his head. "These systems are so encrypted it would take me hours to gain more than the limited access I have to them. We've no idea what's in there so I can't tell you crap. It could take silver bullets, a stake through its heart, UV light, or fragging well anything. There's just no way to know with the scant data we have. Rochester might know but. . ."

The priest was still lost in his prayer as if he was in a trance. Beads of sweat glistened on Rochester's skin. His veins throbbed and tears flowed down over his cheeks. His body shook from the continued fervor of his prayer.

"Damn it," Brack was sick of watching the priest's fit. The priest had to snap out of it for all their sakes.

Brack moved to tower over the priest. Rochester still seemed to have no idea he was even there. Striking out with the butt of his right pistol, Brack knocked the priest over with a vicious blow to his forehead. That did the trick. Rochester sucked in a huge breath like a drowning man breaking the surface of the water he was under. His eyes bugged and then blinked, finally coming to focus on Brack.

"The evil. . ." Rochester muttered. "It's so hungry, so very, very hungry. Don't you feel it?"

"Apparently not like you do," Brack grunted and extended a hand to help the priest back onto his feet. "Sorry about. . ."

"No," Rochester stopped the professional killer's apology. "It had to be done. That thing. . .it nearly overtook me. It reached into my head, cold claws searing my mind. It was. . .it was trying to take me over."

Brack frowned, staring at the priest, not sure how to respond. Was what Rochester telling him real or had the priest experienced a psychotic break?

"It wanted me to kill you both. . .eat you," Rochester whimpered. "Only the power of our savior Jesus Christ saved me."

"Look," Brack gripped the priest firmly by his shoulders, looking into his eyes. "We need to know how to kill this thing and we need to know now, Rochester. Are you getting me?'

"Silver. . ." Rochester managed to get out.

"Silver to its heart."

"Frag me," Brack suddenly realized exactly what kind of metal the corridor they came through was made of now. Looking around, the walls, floors, and ceiling of this room were too. There was silver everywhere but none that could be weaponized. All the three of them had was Rochester's small cross and Brack didn't think for a second that it would be enough to stop the monster inside the tank in its current form.

"He's serious, isn't he?" Marcus asked.

"We must kill it!" Rochester roared, racing towards one of the consoles surrounding the tank. He was hitting buttons and stabbing keys. "There must be a safety feature to eliminate the monster. We just need to find it."

"Stop! You don't know what you're doing!" Marcus squealed in panic, rushing the priest as the shrieks coming from the tank rose in pitch. The young tech slammed into Rochester, sending both of them toppling to the silver floor of the room, a mess of flailing arms and legs. It was too late though. The damage was done.

The tank went dark, its interior lights shutting down. The swirling gray clouds within it gone from their sight. The shrieking stopped too. That unnerved Brack the most. The professional killer ignored the struggle between the tech and the priest. Brack drew his other pistol with lightning speed, facing the tank with both of his guns aimed to fire upon anything that came out of it.

The blast threw Brack through the air like a toy as the side of the tank in front of him exploded outward.

****

Faith and Hemsworth heard all hell break loose on the other side of the Jensen manor as they finally reached its rear. Peter was getting his job done. A couple of the manor's guards emerged from a small security shed ahead of them.

“Down!” Faith whispered harshly at Hemsworth in the bushes that the two of them had been making their way through. Faith was glad they had kept off the main path. If they hadn't, the guards would have spotted them for sure.

“There's one left in there,” Hemsworth whispered back at her after the hurrying guards had passed their position.

“We can handle that,” Faith assured Hemsworth.

"Oh yeah we can," Hemsworth flashed a grin.

The two women crept towards the small security post. Faith wished that Brack was with them. For all her bravado to Hemsworth she was concerned about taking out the single guard without drawing unwanted attention to themselves.

Hemsworth dug in the pocket of her vest and produced a ball-shaped object that at first Faith thought was a grenade. She tossed it into the security post. There was a flash and then the post was instantly filled with gas. The guard came staggering out and collapsed onto the walkway. He lay there, body twitching in violent spasms. . . and then was still.

"Don't worry," Hemsworth assured Faith. "The gas dissipates in a matter of seconds. We can move by there safely."

Impressed, Faith smiled and left the cover of the bushes. There was no sign of other guards around anywhere. An access door that led into the manor's kitchen area was just beyond the post. Faith headed straight for it, heart pounding against her ribs, as she reached the door and took hold of its knob. It turned in her hand and she eased the door open. There were no lights on. Faith stepped into the darkness of the kitchen and motioned to Hemsworth that the room was clear. Faith closed the door behind them. Even if more guards came along outside, there would be no indication that whoever killed the one inside the post had entered the kitchen.

"Which way?" Hemsworth asked, moving to take up a position to the side of the kitchen's exit.

Faith didn't have a ready answer. She'd always planned on having Marcus with them at this point. All he would have needed to do was link into the manor's systems and lead them right to Jensen. . . wherever the bastard was hiding.

She snorted, chiding herself at such a thought. As far as she knew, Jensen didn't hide from anything. It wasn't in the man's nature. Jensen went at things head on with the force and bluntness of a force of nature. That was part of why the bastard had managed to accomplish all the things he had. Part. . . Jensen, as much as Faith hated to admit it, was smart as hell too. She couldn't honestly see him being threatened by an attack on his manor. No. He was ready for them and would be waiting.

"Find us a lift or set of stairs," Faith answered. "Beyond that, it's your call."

Hemsworth nodded and led the two of them out

of the kitchen. There were lights on in the hallways outside of it but they were dim as if they were emergency backups. Was the power to the manor really off? That didn't make any sense. Peter didn't have the firepower or the numbers to have pulled something like that off. Besides, the manor was supposed to have backup systems like the building they had left Brack, Marcus, and Rochester in. Something else had to have happened and what was the million dollar question?

They moved on, as quietly and quickly as possible. Faith could see that the lack of lights was beginning to sink in to Hemsworth too. It was unnerving. Unknowns got you killed and both of them knew it.

"Here!" Hemsworth called out. She had spotted a set of stairs leading up to the manor's second floor. There still was no sign of guards inside the manor at all. That was even more disturbing than the seeming lack of power.

Up the stairs they went with Faith passing Hemsworth to take the sharp end. When they reached the top of them, Faith's gut told her to take a right. She bypassed the other hallways they could have gone down and led them on where her instincts led her.

"This is fragging screwed up, Faith," Hemsworth whispered. "I don't like it."

Faith held up a hand to silence Hemsworth and kept them moving. They came to a set of wide, heavy doors. Something within her told Faith that this had to be where Jensen was. She reached out to try the matching knobs of the doors. They weren't locked and turned in her hands. She gave Hemsworth a sharp nod to let her know to be ready for anything. . . then threw the doors open.

A pistol cracked in the darkness beyond the door. Faith saw the flash of it being fired, barely ducking back in time to avoid a bullet hitting her. Instead, it struck the wood of the heavy door, cracking it but not penetrating.

"It's you, isn't it, Faith?" Jensen shouted from somewhere among the shadows of the room. "Come to get your vengeance for whatever lists of wrongs you've pinned on me? Well, you're too late! We'll all be paying for our sins now."

Faith and Hemsworth traded a confused look. What the hell was going on? Things weren't supposed to go this way no matter how good it was for them. It scared the holy living hell out of Faith.

Jensen's pistol cracked four more times in rapid succession. Each bullet thudded into the doors the two women were using as cover.

“Yeah, Jensen. . .” Faith yelled. “You're damn right it's me. You always knew I would come for you and here I am!”

Faith heard Jensen burst into laughter. “You don't even know what you and your people have done, do you?”

When she didn't answer, Jensen went on. “You’ve let loose hell, girl! Hell on Earth. It'll consume us all and keep right on killing until there's nothing left.”

“What are you talking about, Jensen?” Faith had had enough of his crap. “No. Ya know what? I don't give a flying frag. Drop your damn weapon and come out where we can see you.”

“Or what, Faith?” Jensen said. “You'll come in and get me? I don't think so because if you do, you and yours will get a bullet planted between your eyes.”

“You can't hole up in there forever, Jensen,” Faith replied.

“You didn't listen to anything I said, Faith,” Jensen sounded frustrated. “Don't you get it? We're all dead already. You and your people have seen to that. It'll be coming for us soon and when it does, there's nothing on this Earth that can stop it."

Hemsworth got her attention. "You want me to blow the hell out of him?"

Faith saw the grenade in her hand. She was sure that it wasn't an ordinary one. Hemsworth's hardly ever were. The demo expert liked to make her own suited to specific circumstances. Faith had no doubt that Hemsworth could likely blow this whole side of the manor to bits or set it on fire. Shaking her head, Faith said, "No. Not yet."

"Then what? Are we gonna try to rush him?" Hemsworth's expression made it clear that she thought that was a very bad idea.

"Just hold on," Faith ordered.

Jensen laughed again. "I can hear your bickering. It fits you people. None of your little group are capable of much."

"We got in here and cornered you, didn't we?" Faith countered.

She moved to look around the edge of the door. To her surprise, Jensen didn't take another shot at her. Instead, he emerged from the shadows to stand in front of a window, silhouetted by the moonlight that spilled into the room from the night outside.

"Here I am, Faith," Jensen stared at her. "Why don't you put down that rifle of yours and let's settle all this like it was always meant that we should?"

"Take the shot while you've got it," Hemsworth urged. "Shoot the bastard."

Faith continued to hesitate. Hemsworth swung her rifle to take aim at Jensen. Faith grabbed its barrel. She shoved the barrel upwards while at the same time closing on Hemsworth. With a single strike, Faith sent Hemsworth staggering. The demo expert fell onto her butt, looking up at Faith, completely dumbfounded.

"I am grateful for your help getting here, Hemsworth . . ." Faith told her, "But now, this is between Jensen and myself. Do I make myself clear?"

"Crystal," Hemsworth said and spat blood from where the flat of Faith's palm had struck her face.

Leaving Hemsworth on the floor behind her, Faith marched into the room where Jensen waited. It was time to settle things once and for all.

****

The cloud of gray gas was now spread out all

over the containment room. Rochester and Marcus had stopped their scuffling though it had saved them from the brunt of the blast as the tank exploded. Brack lay on the floor, sucking air back into his lungs. He was bruised badly but nothing had been broken when the explosion flung him across the room like a child's toy. His eyes were wide as he stared at the thing which emerged from what was left of its prison. It stood over seven feet tall and smelled like rotting meat. The yellow orbs of its eyes glowed like miniature suns above a snarling mouth filled with jagged, decaying teeth. The creature looked like a cross between roadkill and a man. Wide antlers topped its skull like those of a deer. The color of its skin was ash gray and utterly unnatural. There were areas where its flesh was eaten away, exposing bone. Though there was no doubt about the power and strength surging through the thing it was sickeningly gaunt and Brack could feel its hunger in the depths of his very soul. Brack's mind screamed the same word over and over again in primal terror - Wendigo! Wendigo! Wendigo!

Rochester and Marcus moved to engage the monster. Brack was too stunned to join them. He'd fought many creatures in his career but nothing ever like the entity before him now. The sheer power of its presence locked his muscles and froze him in fear. How the others were able to do anything, much less fight it, was beyond Brack's understanding.

Marcus fumbled his attempt to draw the pistol holstered on his hip. His hands were just too badly damaged. It clanked onto the metal floor while Rochester charged the monster. He held the silver cross in his right hand like a dagger, stabbing its bottom in the creature's chest. The Wendigo squealed in pain, ash gray flesh smoking where the silver of the cross pierced its body. Its feet were smoking as well where they touched the room's floor. Small tendrils twisted upwards towards the room's ceiling. The monster lashed out at the priest, delivering a backhanded blow to Rochester that lifted him from his feet. The priest was flung across the room, smashing into its far wall. His body bounced off of it to land with Rochester's head bent at an unnatural angle, white bone of his spine poking through and protruding from the base of his neck.

The monster turned its attention to Marcus next. The young tech cried out as the great, gaunt beast stomped across the silver floor, closing in on him.

Marcus retreated behind one of the room's control consoles, smashing the gauntlet-like computer pad of his arm down onto its screen. Sparks flew as the glass shattered. Ignoring how much it hurt, Marcus thrust an injured hand into the wires making sure the console caught on fire. The Wendigo shrieked in anger, backpedaling a single step. Its yellow eyes glared at the young tech.

"Fire hurts it too!" Marcus shouted at him as Brack finally began to pull himself together.

The young tech apparently thought the blazing console would keep the Wendigo at bay on the other side of it. Unfortunately for him, that wasn't the case. The creature darted forward, around the console, giving the flames a wide berth. One of its skeletal hands shot out to close around Marcus's neck. The young tech was lifted off the floor in its grasp. Marcus's legs kicked about in the air as he pounded the arm that held him with his wounded hands. With a simple flick of its thumb, the monster snapped Marcus's neck and stood there holding his corpse. The gaunt thing didn't let the young tech's body drop to the floor though. Instead, its jaw unhinged as it shoved Marcus's entire head into the open maw of its mouth. The creature bit down, severing Marcus's head in an explosion of hot, wet redness. Brack heard the crunch as the monster chewed upon the young tech's skull. Only then did the Wendigo fling Marcus's body away.

Rochester and Marcus had bought Brack the time he needed to at least somewhat recover from the supernatural terror that had overwhelmed him when the monster broke free. He leaped to his feet, twin pistols barking. One boomed then the other as Brack put five rounds into the Wendigo's chest. They appeared to have no effect whatsoever. He couldn't tell if the thing had gone incorporeal like the wind itself or if the bullets were merely being swallowed up harmlessly by its ash gray flesh and aura of hunger. Brack switched tactics quickly, like the professional killer he was. His next two shots thudded into the monster's knees. His hope was to blow out the joints in them and render the creature less mobile. They had as little effect as his first shots. The Wendigo seemed to be sneering at him through it all.

“Die, damn you!” Brack yelled, switching his aim again. This time, he put rounds into both of the Wendigo's yellow eyes. The yellow orbs burst as they were crushed within their sockets, a foul black fluid squirting out as the bullets entered. Lids closed over the mess of the creature's eyes as it shook in fury. Brack didn't let up, pouring more rounds into the monster, emptying his pistols into its chest and stomach. When the gunfire stopped, his weapons clicking empty, the Wendigo opened its eyes. They were completely whole once more and glowing with yellow rage.

Brack threw his empty pistols at the gaunt creature lunging at him. Twisting sideways, he narrowly avoided its attack for all the good it did him. The Wendigo whirled around with impossible speed, grabbing Brack from behind. It turned him in its grasp so that their eyes met. Brack tried to close his but found he couldn't. His gaze was locked to that of the Wendigo's. The thing's yellow eyes felt as if they were burrowing, burning into his mind. Brack opened his mouth to scream but in that moment, the Wendigo became a foul, putrid fog-like mist and thrust itself down his throat.

****

Peter and Finn were met by Jones and Winston at the garages just inside the manor's main gates. There were no more sounds of gunfire. The guards pursuing them appeared to have broken off. Peter couldn't explain it. The estate's alarms had fallen silent as well.

“What's going on?” Winston snarled.

“Not a fragging clue,” Peter answered honestly. There was no explanation for it all. The guards had the firepower and the numbers. He and the others were on the run. With the element of surprise gone, they couldn't make a stand against them like they had planned without likely sentencing themselves to death in the process.

“I know I have a head injury but why would they stop? They were about to have us dead to rights,” Finn said.

“Wait,” Jones held up a hand. “Do you guys smell that?”

Winston's nose turned up as the odor hit him. Peter smelt it too.

“Frag me,” Finn shook her head. “That's rancid.”

And the smell was. It stank of soured blood.

They all heard the creatures before the things came into sight, bounding towards them from the bushes. Their snarls were deep and guttural in contrast to their size. The things were small, no more than three or four feet high, running on all fours like a bear. Rows of spikes ran the lengths of their backs from the base of their necks to their tails.

"Chupacabras!" Winston shouted.

"Frag! They're using the things like dogs!" Peter yelled. "Take the bastards out!"

The group opened fire on the approaching monsters. Winston was using his combat shotgun again. The heavy weapon unleashed a chorus of thunderclaps as the ex-farmer-turned-solider fired it on semi-auto, targeting one of the goat suckers then another, making sure each shot counted. The Chupacabras were no Sasquatch. Each one Winston hit blew apart in a shower of red gore from the power of the round hitting them. Peter let loose with his AK-47 on full auto, spraying the snarling pack that was closing on them far too fast. Finn and Jones were firing too but even so, it just wasn't enough to break the Chupacbras' charge. Several of the dog-like beasts dropped, bodies torn and mangled by the barrage of automatic fire being poured into them.

The Chupacabras reached Peter and the others. One of the things leaped onto Jones, taking the hardened mechanic to the ground. Its long tongue stabbed outward plunging into the center of her throat. A sickening wheezing noise came from Jones as the thing sucked the blood out of her.

"No!" Finn shouted, flinging her rifle away to draw the sword sheathed on her back. The swordswoman rushed the Chupacabra holding Jones down. She swung, the blade of her sword slashing a deep gash along the monster's side. The Chupacabra squealed in pain, withdrawing its long tongue from Jones's throat. Blood spurted from the open hole in Jones's neck as her body jerked about in its death throes. Seeing that she had acted too late to save Jones, Finn took out her anger on the beast that killed her friend. Finn struck again, her blade severing the Chupacabra's head.

Winston's combat shotgun thundered sending another Chupacabra back to whatever hell the thing had crawled out of. He started to fall back to reload but with Finn and Jones busy, there was only Peter left to cover him and Peter had his own hands full. A trio of the creatures swarmed Winston, claws raking at his flesh. Blood flew from the wounds they opened up on his chest, legs, and arms. Winston slammed the butt of his shotgun into the mouth of a Chupacabra that leapt to take him down, breaking its jaw. The beast was knocked sideways.

Winston had no time to finish it. The other two were still at him, one in front, one behind. Claws ran over the length of his back, tearing meat away from his spine. The monster in front of him shot out its tongue. Its razor-tipped end thudded into Winston's forehead, breaking through the bone of his skull. Winston's world went instantly black before his eyes and for him, the fight was over.

Peter saw Jones and Winston die. There wasn't a damn thing he could do about it. He was engaged with a Chupacabra that clutched his AK-47 in its paw-like hands. The two of them wrestled, each trying to get the weapon away from the other. Peter was taller and larger than the creature but despite its size, the thing was just as strong as he was. It won the battle, wrenching the rifle from his grasp. Drawing his sidearm, Peter fired it three times. Each round punched a hole in the Chupacabra's chest, sending it reeling backwards. A fourth shot sent the beast's brains splattering out from the backside of its skull. The thing's corpse toppled to the ground in front of Peter.

Finn's blade opened up the guts of a Chupacabra as it jumped for her and she ducked beneath the beast. Its foul blood rained down over her. Finn rose back to her feet moving to spear the wounded creature with her sword before it could even try to get up from where it had landed. She and Peter were fighting the good fight and giving them hell but there were just too many of the fragging things. Finn spun about as yet another charged her. Her sword split the monster's long snout into two halves. The Chupacabra's momentum carried it on to collide with her though. Finn grunted as the breath was knocked from her lungs and she was sent stumbling by the impact. The monsters gave her no time to recover. One of them was on her back in the span of a heartbeat. Its claws dug into her shoulders, holding onto Finn. She tried to shake it loose but the thing's long tongue flicked out from its mouth, burying itself deep into her brain.

"No!" Peter cried out. Finn's body fell with the Chupacabra still sucking blood and brain matter from her. Now, he was alone. Peter had figured drawing attention away so that Faith and the others could slip into Jensen's manor would be suicide but never thought it would be fragging monsters that killed them all. He'd expected to die in a furious firefight not having his blood sucked from his veins.

Peter emptied his pistol into a Chupacabra that

rushed him from his left and turned around as another came at him from his right. He met the monster with a kick to its snout. The Chupacabra grunted, brought to a sharp halt. Peter knew he couldn't fight the thing without a weapon so he ran. Legs pumping under him, Peter sprinted for the closest of the garages. Before he reached it, the main door rose up, revealing a pair of Jensen's security people. Their weapons were leveled at his chest as they opened fire. Peter died screaming.

****

Faith and Jensen faced each other like Old West gunfighters. Hemsworth heaved herself up from the floor where she lay just beyond the doorway of the room they were in as Faith made her move. She snapped her right leg up in a high kick aimed at his chin. Jensen parried the attack with one arm, grabbing her with his other hand. Though he couldn't hold onto her, it was enough to throw Faith off balance. She fell to the floor with a loud thud. Jensen rushed her but Faith rolled in time to avoid his foot coming down on her chest. Faith came up on her feet, taking a swing at Jensen. It crashed into the side of his head. Before Jensen could recover from that blow, Faith kicked out, breaking his right leg at the knee. Jensen wailed in pain and collapsed. Faith stood towering over him.

"You had enough yet?" she asked.

"Does it matter?" Jensen snarled.

Faith, smiling, kicked Jensen in the mouth. Jensen spat teeth and blood.

"Uh. . .Faith," Hemsworth shouted from the doorway. "Someone's coming up the steps!"

"Deal with them, damn it," Faith barked.

"I. . .I think it's Brack," Hemsworth stammered.

"It's not Brack," Jensen laughed.

Hemsworth screamed. It was the high-pitched cry of a woman dying in unimaginable pain.

Faith and Jensen were both watching the doorway as something in the shape of a man entered the room. It was wearing Brack's body but like Jensen had said, it wasn't him. Brack's skin was taut and pulled tight against his bones. His eyes burnt yellow in the shadows of the room. Hemsworth's decapitated head was clutched by its hair in his left hand.

"God help me," Faith muttered. She retreated as the thing sprang at them.

Faith got clear of its reach but saw that the thing

had been going for Jensen where he lay on the floor and not her. Its hands held Jensen tight as Brack's newly jagged teeth ripped out his throat. Hot blood sprayed over Brack's chin and cheeks as his head rose up with a piece of Jensen's flesh in his mouth.

Through the doorway came more things like Brack. All of them gaunt, skeletal figures with blazing yellow eyes like his. She could see even more of them beyond those that had entered.

Faith drew the pistol holstered on her hip. She'd no intention of using it on Jensen but these creatures were another matter. Wishing she hadn't left her rifle outside with Hemsworth, Faith took aim at Brack as the monster he had became rose up from where it had finished mauling Jensen.

"Thank you, Faith," Brack rasped in a voice that was no longer human. It was cold, so cold that the sound of it sent shivers running through her body. The hairs on the back of her neck stood up in response to the primal fear that the thing in front of her filled Faith with.

"What. . . what are you?" Faith asked.

"Oh, Faith. . ." The thing that wore Brack's body clicked its tongue, wiping Jensen's blood from its mouth with the backside of a hand. "I am the end."

"Stay the hell away from me," Faith warned, her pistol extended towards the foul creature in a two handed grip.

"Your hunger for vengeance is like my hunger, Faith," the thing purred. "Even now, though Jensen lies dead, you long to hurt him more. You were my instrument, my tool with which to be freed upon the world."

"Frag you," Faith growled and pulled the trigger of her pistol. The gun barked three times putting a trio of bullets into the center of Brack's chest. A putrid, foul substance exploded outward instead of blood where each buried itself into him. Aside from that, the bullets didn't seem to affect the thing that Brack had become at all. It stepped closer to Faith. She could smell its breath. Her stomach emptied its contents as Faith bent to vomit all over her own feet. In that instant, Brack shot forward to take hold of her. Faith's head jerked upwards and she found herself looking directly into his burning, yellow eyes.

With a quick, easy movement, Brack yanked her head to him. Their mouths met in a kiss that sealed Faith's fate. Faith struggled against the thing that was Brack as unearthly, unholy cold poured into her.

. . then it was over. All she felt was hunger. When Brack released her, Faith's eyes glowed yellow too.

“And now,” Brack cackled, licking his lips hungrily, “It's the world's turn.”

The End

Author Bio

Eric S Brown is the author of numerous book series including the Bigfoot War series, the Psi-Mechs Inc. series, the Kaiju Apocalypse series (with Jason Cordova), the Crypto-Squad series (with Jason Brannon), the Homeworld series (With Tony Faville and Jason Cordova), the Jack Bunny Bam series, and the A Pack of Wolves series. Some of his stand alone books include War of the Worlds plus Blood Guts and Zombies, Casper Alamo (with Jason Brannon), Sasquatch Island, Day of the Sasquatch, Bigfoot, Crashed, World War of the Dead, Last Stand in a Dead Land, Sasquatch Lake, Kaiju Armageddon, Megalodon, Megalodon Apocalypse, Kraken, Alien Battalion, The Last Fleet, and From the Snow They Came to name only a few. His short fiction has been published hundreds of times in the small press in beyond including markets like the Onward Drake and Black Tide Rising anthologies from Baen Books, the Grantville Gazette, the SNAFU Military horror anthology series, and Walmart World magazine. He has done the novelizations for such films as Boggy Creek: The

Legend is True (Studio 3 Entertainment) and The Bloody Rage of Bigfoot (Great Lake films). The first book of his Bigfoot War series was adapted into a feature film by Origin Releasing in 2014. Werewolf Massacre at Hell's Gate was the second of his books to be adapted into film in 2015. Major Japanese publisher, Takeshobo, bought the reprint rights to his Kaiju Apocalypse series (with Jason Cordova) and the mass market, Japanese language version was released in late 2017. Ring of Fire Press has released a collected edition of his Monster Society stories (set in the New York Times Best-selling world of Eric Flint's 1632). In addition to his fiction, Eric also writes an award-winning comic book news column entitled "Comics in a Flash" as well a pop culture column for Altered Reality Magazine. Eric lives in North Carolina with his wife and two children where he continues to write tales of the hungry dead, blazing guns, and the things that lurk in the woods.

Check out other great

Cryptid Novels!

J.H. Moncrieff

RETURN TO DYATLOV PASS

In 1959, nine Russian students set off on a skiing expedition in the Ural Mountains. Their mutilated bodies were discovered weeks later. Their bizarre and unexplained deaths are one of the most enduring true mysteries of our time. Nearly sixty years later, podcast host Nat McPherson ventures into the same mountains with her team, determined to finally solve the mystery of the Dyatlov Pass incident. Her plans are thwarted on the first night, when two trackers from her group are brutally slaughtered. The team's guide, a superstitious man from a neighboring village, blames the killings on yetis, but no one believes him. As members of Nat's team die one by one, she must figure out if there's a murderer in their midst—or something even worse—before history repeats itself and her group becomes another casualty of the infamous Dead Mountain.

Gerry Griffiths

CRYPTID ZOO

As a child, rare and unusual animals, especially cryptid creatures, always fascinated Carter Wilde. Now that he's an eccentric billionaire and runs the largest conglomerate of high-tech companies all over the world, he can finally achieve his wildest dream of building the most incredible theme park ever conceived on the planet... CRYPTID ZOO. Even though there have been apparent problems with the project, Wilde still decides to send some of his marketing employees and their families on a forced vacation to assess the theme park in preparation for Opening Day. Nick Wells and his family are some of those chosen and are about to embark on what will become the most terror-filled weekend of their lives—praying they survive. STEP RIGHT UP AND GET YOUR FREE PASS... TO CRYPTID ZOO

Check out other great

Cryptid Novels!

P.K. Hawkins

THE CRYPTID FILES

Fresh out of the academy with top marks, Agent Bradley Tennyson is expecting to have the pick of cases and investigations throughout the country. So he's shocked when instead he is assigned as the new partner to "The Crag," an agent well past his prime. He thinks the assignment is a punishment. It's anything but.Agent George Crag has been doing this job for far longer than most, and he knows what skeletons his bosses have in the closet and where the bodies are buried. He has pretty much free reign to pick his cases, and he knows exactly which one he wants to use to break in his new young partner: the disappearance and murder of a couple of college kids in a remote mountain town.Tennyson doesn't realize it, but Crag is about to introduce him to a world he never believed existed: The Cryptid Files, a world of strange monsters roaming in the night. Because these murders have been going on for a long time, and evidence is mounting that the murderer may just in fact be the legendary Bigfoot.

Gerry Griffiths

DOWN FROM BEAST MOUNTAIN

A beast with a grudge has come down from the mountain to terrorize the townsfolk of Porterville. The once sleepy town is suddenly wide awake. Sheriff Abel McGuire and game warden Grant Tanner frantically investigate one brutal slaying after another as they follow the blood trail they hope will eventually lead to the monstrous killer. But they better hurry and stop the carnage before the census taker has to come out and change the population sign on the edge of town to ZERO.

www.ingramcontent.com/pod-product-compliance
Lightning Source LLC
Chambersburg PA
CBHW061243170626
46809CB00007B/2805